Emily.

Cat
the |

A PLAY IN THREE ACTS

By Georges Feydeau

Translated by John Mortimer

A SAMUEL FRENCH ACTING EDITION

SAMUEL FRENCH

FOUNDED 1830

New York Hollywood London Toronto

SAMUELFRENCH.COM

Produced by H. M. Tennent Limited and Bernard Delfont at Wimbledon on the 17th March 1969, and subsequently at the Prince of Wales Theatre, London, on the 15th April 1969, with the following cast of characters:

(In the Order of Their Appearance)

MARCELINE	*Rosemary Martin*
FIRMIN	*Jay Denyer*
LUCETTE GAUTIER	*Elizabeth Seal*
GONTRAN DE CHENNEVIETTE	*John Hart Dyke*
NINI GALANT	*Miranda Marshall*
FERNAND BOIS D'ENGHIEN	*Richard Briers*
IGNACE DE FONTANET	*Peter Gray*
BARONESS DUVERGER	*Helen Christie*
CAMILLE BOUZIN	*Murray Melvin*
GENERAL IRRIGUA	*Victor Spinetti*
ANTONIO, *the Interpreter*	*Richard Dennis*
VIVIANE	*Sheila Davies*
FRAULEIN FITZENSPIEGEL	*Daphne Newton*
EMILE, *servant to the Baroness*	*Paul Hastings*
LANTERY, *a solicitor*	*Richard Young*
JEAN, *a valet*	*Richard Dennis*
FLOWER BOY	*Graham Edwards*
MAN, *wedding guest*	*Richard Young*
WOMAN, *wedding guest*	*Jacqueline Lacey*
LE CONCIERGE	*Jay Denyer*
POLICEMEN	*Paul Hastings, John Bromley*

WEDDING PARTY AND GUESTS:
Rose Alba, Miranda Hampton, Venessa Kempster, Olga Bennett, Darryl Kavann, Stanley Lloyd, Patrick Marley, Douglas Ridley

3

Directed by JACQUES CHARON
Designed by ANDRÉ LEVASSEUR

ACT I: Lucette's Drawing Room

ACT II: Baroness Duverger's Bedroom

ACT III: Bois d'Enghien's Apartment

Cat Among The Pigeons

ACT ONE

SCENE: LUCETTE'S *drawing room. The room is elegantly furnished.* U. S. *the Left wall is parallel to the Right wall. Then it meets a section of wall at Right angles to it.* U. L. *is a door leading to* LUCETTE'S *bedroom.* B. S. *there are two doors. They open into the room. The one* B. L. C. *leads to the dining room. The other* B. R. C. *leads to an entrance hall. Against the back wall of the entrance hall is a wardrobe. Against the back wall of the dining room is a sideboard crowded with tableware. Against the right-angled* L. *wall is a draped mantelpiece, over it an ornate mirror.* U. S. R. *is another door.* (NOTE: all the doors are double doors.) R. *a piano with its back to the wall and a stool in front of it.* D. L. *a console table with an empty vase on it.* R. *near the piano, but with sufficient room to pass between the two pieces of furniture, a sofa with its back to the piano and almost perpendicular to the set* R. *of the sofa is a small round table.* L. *of the sofa is a wing chair.* L. *at an angle to the console table is a medium sized rectangular table with chairs* L., R. *and behind it. There is a pouf or small footstool in front of the fireplace.* R. *of the fireplace a chair against the wall.* B. S. C. *between the two doors a bureau with drawers. Knick knacks everywhere. Vases on the mantelpiece. Pictures on the walls. A folded copy of* LE FIGARO *lies on the table* R.

At the rise of the CURTAIN, MARCELINE *is standing by the fireplace, her right arm resting on the mantel-*

5

piece, drumming her fingers, waiting impatiently.
FIRMIN, *who is finishing laying the dining room table,*
looks at his watch.

MARCELINE. For goodness sake, Firmin, if you don't
serve lunch soon, I'm going to drop dead. (*She crosses to*
chair R.)

FIRMIN. You'll get it the moment she wakes up.

MARCELINE. You mean—gets out of bed . . .

FIRMIN. And not a moment before. (*He crosses* U. S. *to*
dining room doors.)

MARCELINE. (*She crosses to sofa and sits.*) Now
M'sieur Bois d'Enghien's left her, I can't see why my
little sister has to hang about in the bedroom all by herself.

FIRMIN. (*He crosses* D. S. *level with* MARCELINE.) Perhaps she's entertaining someone we don't know about?

MARCELINE. Don't be silly. There isn't anyone we
don't know about.

FIRMIN. That's true.

MARCELINE. And even when her lover *was* here, in the
old days . . .

FIRMIN. Two weeks ago . . .

MARCELINE. I never understood why Lucette couldn't
be absolutely dotty about the chap and still get up for
lunch. (*She rises and crosses to the* L. *of* FIRMIN.) Or
does love make one totally oblivious of time? Of course,
I've had no personal experience . . .

FIRMIN. Too bad . . .

MARCELINE. Speaking entirely as a virgin . . .

FIRMIN. I know!

MARCELINE. (*She crosses to the sofa and sits.*) No
one wants to take on the elder sister of a Music Hall
Artiste. (FIRMIN *crosses* U. S. *towards the dining room.*)
But what I always say is—look at the cock. (FIRMIN
stops in his tracks and turns.) Busy all night among the
hens, and up bright as a button at four o'clock in the
morning.

FIRMIN. It's different with us theatricals . . .

(LUCETTE *enters quickly from the bedroom, closes the door and crosses* C., *then* D. S. *to the chair* L. *of the table and sits.* FIRMIN *crosses to* U. S. *dining room doors on the closing of the bedroom door by* LUCETTE.)

LUCETTE. Marceline!

MARCELINE. (*She rises and crosses to* LUCETTE.) Lucette . . . At last!

LUCETTE. (*Radiant.*) I feel absolutely marvellous. He's back! (*She sits* R. *of the table.*)

MARCELINE. M'sieur Bois d'Enghien? No!

LUCETTE. M'sieur Bois d'Enghien! Yes!

MARCELINE. (*She crosses* U. S. *to* FIRMIN.) Oh, Firmin! M'sieur Bois d'Enghien's back!

FIRMIN. (*He crosses slightly to* LUCETTE *then back to* U. S.) M'sieur Bois d'Enghien. That'll improve her temper.

(MARCELINE *crosses* D. S. C.)

LUCETTE. (*Rising, delighted.*) Poor boy. He explained it all last night. When I accused him of loving someone else he fainted dead away for two weeks.

MARCELINE. (*Moves a little to the* R.) How ghastly!

LUCETTE. It doesn't bear thinking about! Suppose he'd never regained the use of his . . .

MARCELINE. Legs?

LUCETTE. (*She crosses* U. S. R. *to* R. *of* FIRMIN, FIRMIN *moves towards her a little.*) Exactly! (*To* FIRMIN.) He's so beautiful! Firmin—you have noticed that, haven't you?

FIRMIN. (*Not having heard the conversation moves* D. S. *a little.*) Noticed what?

MARCELINE. How beautiful M'sieur Bois d'Enghien is.

FIRMIN. (*Unconvinced.*) Oh, perfectly gorgeous. (*He crosses* U. S. *to the dining room.*)

LUCETTE. (*She crosses* D. S. *to* U. R. *of* MARCELINE.) I adore him.

BOIS D'ENG. (*Offstage calling.*) Lucette!

LUCETTE. That's him! He's calling me! (*To* MARCELINE.) You remember the voice? (*She crosses* U. S. *to door* R.)

MARCELINE. How could I forget it . . . ? (*She crosses to the* L. *of* LUCETTE.)

LUCETTE. (*By the bedroom door.*) I'm here, darling.

(FIRMIN *crosses to the* L. *of* MARCELINE.)

MARCELINE. (*Moving towards the bedroom.*) Can we have a peep at him?

LUCETTE. Yes, of course! Fernand! (*She's by the door, speaking Offstage to* BOIS D'ENGHIEN.) Marceline wants to say hullo to you!

BOIS D'ENG. (*Offstage.*) Hullo Marceline!

MARCELINE. (*By the fireplace.*) Hullo M'sieur Fernand!

FIRMIN. (*Behind* MARCELINE.) Everything all right, M'sieur Fernand?

BOIS D'ENG. (*Offstage.*) Is that you, Firmin? Not bad . . . Just a slight headache.

MARCELINE. ⎫
FIRMIN. ⎭ Oh . . . What a shame!

LUCETTE. (*Going towards the bedroom.*) Get dressed, darling. We're going to have lunch. (*She exits to the bedroom.*)

MARCELINE. At last!

(*DOORBELL.*)

FIRMIN. I'm coming. (*He crosses* U. S. L. *and through the doors, not closing them, and off.*)

MARCELINE. (*She crosses* D. S. *to chair* L. *of table and sits.*) Hurry up! I'm dying of hunger.

FIRMIN. (*Offstage.*) M'sieur de Chenneviette . . .

DE CHENNEV. (*Offstage.*) Good morning, Firmin.

(DE CHENNEVIETTE *enters* U. S. *and is followed by*
FIRMIN *who places his hat and coat on the hat stand,
and then shows* DE CHENNEVIETTE *into the room.*)

FIRMIN. (*He crosses down* C.) M'sieur de Chenneviette.
(*To* DE CHENNEVIETTE.) Just dropped in for lunch, have
you?

(DE CHENNEVIETTE *crosses* D. L. *to the sofa, taking off
his gloves and placing them on the table* D. R. *Takes
cigar out of box.*)

DE CHENNEV. Naturally.
FIRMIN. (*Sarcastically.*) Naturally!
DE CHENNEV. (*Without going to her.*) How are you,
Marceline?
MARCELINE. (*Sulky.*) Dying.
FIRMIN. (*He crosses* D. C. *level with the chair* R. *of the
sofa.*) Have you heard the news? He's back!
DE CHENNEV. Who's back?
MARCELINE. M'sieur Bois d'Enghien!
DE CHENNEV. (*Shuts cigar box.*) I don't believe it!
FIRMIN. (*He crosses to door* R.) Large as life.
DE CHENNEV. (*Shrugs his shoulders.*) And penniless as
ever?
FIRMIN. I'll announce the fact you've come to lunch as
usual . . .

(MARCELINE *rises and crosses* U. S. *to* U. S. R. *doors.*)

DE CHENNEV. What's the matter with him? He knows
I always come on Fridays . . . For the oysters . . .

(FIRMIN *knocks at* LUCETTE's *door.*)

FIRMIN. Madame.

LUCETTE. (*Offstage.*) What is it?

FIRMIN. It's M'sieur.

LUCETTE. M'sieur who?

FIRMIN. (*In one breath.*) Monsieur-the-father-of-Madame's-child.

LUCETTE. All right. I'm coming.

FIRMIN. (*To* DE CHENNEVIETTE *without moving.*) She's coming!

DE CHENNEV. Oh good. (FIRMIN *crosses to* U. S. R. *doors and into the dining room.*) So Fernand's back . . .

(MARCELINE *crosses* D. S. C. *level with* DE CHEN-NEVIETTE.)

MARCELINE. (*Meaning look at* LUCETTE'S *door, then she crosses* R. *to chair* L. *of table and sits.*) She announced it as if it were the 14th of July.

DE CHENNEV. He's a nice boy, but he can't really afford her . . .

MARCELINE. She says all really attractive men love beyond their means. I don't know anything about that, of course—speaking as a virgin naturally . . .

DE CHENNEV. Naturally. (*Remembering something.*) What's happened to Lucette's gorgeous Mexican?

MARCELINE. Oh, he's been postponed indefinitely.

DE CHENNEV. General Irrigua? Apparently he sits in the theatre watching her with a glint in his eye.

MARCELINE. You mean a genuine 24 carat glint . . . ?

DE CHENNEV. Anyway, she gave the General permission to come and introduce himself this afternoon. But now Prince Charming's in residence, the meeting could be embarrassing.

MARCELINE. To say the least . . .

(*DOORBELL.* FIRMIN *crosses to the doors* U. S. L. MAR-CELINE *and* DE CHENNEVIETTE *rise.*)

FIRMIN. Not someone else! Good morning Mademoiselle Nini . . .

NINI. (*Offstage.*) Good morning, Firmin . . .

(FIRMIN *lets in* NINI GALANT. *He crosses to* U. S. C. *followed by* NINI GALANT, *he closes the* U. S. L. *doors.*)

FIRMIN. Come in, Mademoiselle . . .
MARCELINE.
DE CHENNEV. } Nini Galant!

(NINI *crosses* D. S. *to between the sofa and the chair.*)

NINI. In the flesh! (*She puts her things on the sofa near the chair and moves* D. S.) How's everyone? (*She crosses* D. L. *of* MARCELINE *and kisses her.*) Marceline, darling! Still a virgin?
MARCELINE. Nothing changes . . .
NINI. Give it up darling, you're putting on weight. (*She crosses* C. *waving to* DE CHENNEVIETTE, *turns to end up between the sofa and the chair. To* DE CHEN-NEVIETTE.) Come for the oysters?
FIRMIN. You've heard the news, Mademoiselle?
NINI. I've heard my news. What's your news . . . ?
EVERYONE. He's back!
NINI. Who's back?
EVERYONE. M'sieur Bois d'Enghien!

(FIRMIN *crosses into the dining room.*)

NINI. You're joking!

(LUCETTE *enters* R. *and crosses* D. S. *to below the chair* L. *of the table.*)

LUCETTE. Nini darling! (NINI *crosses* D. R. *to* L. *of* LUCETTE *and kisses her.*) Been working, darling?
NINI. Night and day!
LUCETTE. (*To* DE CHENNEVIETTE.) Hullo Gontran . . .

(*She crosses* D. L. *to* DE CHENNEVIETTE.) Darlings . . .
You've heard the wonderful news?

NINI. (*She crosses to the* R. *of* LUCETTE.) They told
me! Marvellous for you, darling! He must feel like a new
lover since he had all those nights off . . .

LUCETTE. He's in *there* . . .

NINI. You keep him in there, darling! Once you let
them out, they're inclined to wander off . . .

LUCETTE. (*Crossing to below* NINI *to door* R.—NINI
to LUCETTE'S L., MARCELINE *to* NINI'S L.) Wait . . .
(FIRMIN *crosses to* L. *of* MARCELINE, *slightly* U. S.) I'll
show him to you. (DE CHENNEVIETTE *crosses* U. S. *to
below* C. *chair.* LUCETTE *goes to the door* L.) Fernand.
It's Nini. What? Oh, just come as you are, darling. It's
quite informal . . . I mean . . . Everyone *knows* you.
(*To the others.*) And . . . Ladies and Gentlemen. It's
my great pleasure to introduce . . . Back! By special re-
quest! Your friend and my friend, Fernand Bois
d'Enghien! (*They all turn to form a diagonal line towards
the bedroom door as* BOIS D'ENGHIEN *enters—dressed in
a magnificent dressing gown, from the door* R. *He greets*
EVERYONE *in turn.*) Hi . . . Hip . . . Hip . . .

EVERYONE. Hurray!

BOIS D'ENG. (*Modestly, acknowledging the cheers.*)
Oh, Ladies and Gentlemen . . .

(*The following dialogue is very quick.* FIRMIN *crosses*
D. R. *to* R. *of table.*)

NINI. The Wandering Lover . . .
BOIS D'ENG. What? Well, you see I . . .
MARCELINE. He's dreadful . . . But we all adore him.
BOIS D'ENG. (*Modestly.*) Oh . . . do you really . . . ?
DE CHENNEV. Nice to see you again.
BOIS D'ENG. . . . Thanks, old fellow.
FIRMIN. (*He crosses* R. *to* BOIS D'ENGHIEN.) She had to
hook up her own dresses while you were away . . . She
said it got very lonely.

Bois d'Eng. (*Shaking hands all round.*) Did she really?

Everyone. He's back, Lucette! That's the great thing.

(Firmin *exits through doors* u. s. r. *End of very quick dialogue.*)

Bois d'Eng. (*Smiling.*) By God yes. I'm back! To say the least! (*Moves* l. *and sadly brushes his hair.*) Isn't it splendid . . . ? And I only called in to break it off. I'm marrying someone else. (*He sits down, disconsolate, on the* r. *of the table.*)

(De Chenneviette *crosses to behind* l. *of sofa,* Nini *to* u. s. *of sofa and sits.* Lucette *sits on the chair* c. Marceline *sits* d. s. *end of sofa.*)

Lucette. (*To* Nini.) Stay for lunch, darling.

Nini. No, honestly . . . I just came to tell you—I can't stay!

Lucette. Tell him to bring in the oysters . . .

Marceline. Without a moment's delay . . .

(Marceline *crosses* u. s. r. *and goes into the dining room.* De Chenneviette *crosses to the* r. *of* Lucette.)

Lucette. Why can't you stay, Nini?

Nini. (*She moves to the* c. *of the sofa and turns to* Lucette.) Because of my news! I've got news too. . . . Stupendous . . . Fabulous . . . Unbelievable news! I'm getting married, my darling.

Lucette.
De Chennev. } *You,* darling . . . ?

Bois d'Eng. You, darling . . . ? (*Aside.*) That makes two of us. (*He sits on chair* r. *of table.*)

Nini. Little me! He's terribly upper class.

Lucette. Nothing but the best for Nini.

De Chennev. Who is this fearless character?

bitchy

NINI. My lover!

DE CHENNEV. You're marrying your lover? Then where on earth will you go in the afternoons?

NINI. Don't be rude!

LUCETTE. Excuse me; which lover, darling?

NINI. The best one! I'm going to be Duchesse de la Courbelle!

LUCETTE. You'll be seen all over Paris.

DE CHENNEV. Like the Eiffel Tower?

LUCETTE. You'll still have to pay to be shown round her, darling!

(BOIS D'ENGHIEN *who has been looking through* Figaro *lying beside him jumps to his feet and faces* D. S.)

girly talk with Lucette

BOIS D'ENG. Oh my God! They announced my engagement in the *Figaro*. (*He crumples up the paper and stuffs it under his dressing gown and holds it to his breast.*)

LUCETTE. (*She rises and faces* BOIS D'ENGHIEN.) What's the matter, darling?

BOIS D'ENG. Nothing, darling. A touch of heartburn . . .

LUCETTE. (*She moves towards* BOIS D'ENGHIEN.) You're not going to faint again, sweetheart?

BOIS D'ENG. Of course not. (LUCETTE *crosses back to the chair* C. *and sits. She whispers loudly to* NINI *about* BOIS D'ENGHIEN'S *illness.*) It's disgraceful! Without a word of warning . . . Your forthcoming marriage creeps up and punches you in the breadbasket!

DE CHENNEV. Lucette. Have you read your wonderful review in this morning's *Figaro?*

LUCETTE. No.

DE CHENNEV. I've got it here. (*He takes a copy of the* Figaro *out of his pocket and opens it.*)

BOIS D'ENG. (*He crosses to* R. *of* DE CHENNEVIETTE.) What've you got there?

DE CHENNEV. Like to read it?

(BOIS D'ENGHIEN *rushes at* DE CHENNEVIETTE *and snatches the paper from him. He then crosses to below the table* R.)

BOIS D'ENG. Not at the moment! Thank you very much! (*He stuffs the second newspaper into the same place as the first.*)

(LUCETTE *and* MARCELINE *rise.*)

EVERYONE. *What . . . ?*
BOIS D'ENG. It's lunchtime! Hardly the time to sit round reading newspapers . . .
DE CHENNEV. (*He crosses to the chair* L. *of table.*) He's not well . . .
MARCELINE. (*She enters* U. S.) It's ready! (*She exits* U. S.)
BOIS D'ENG. You see? It's ready!
DE CHENNEV. He's certainly not well . . . (*He crosses* C.)

(*The BELL RINGS.*) ~~frauy crosses~~

BOIS D'ENG. (*Going to the door on the* L. *Aside as he goes.*) Where's my strength of character? I swear I'll break it to her after the crepe suzette! (*He crosses* U. S. *above the table, carrying his hair brush.*)

(DE CHENNEVIETTE *crosses* U. S. *of* LUCETTE.)

LUCETTE. (*To* BOIS D'ENGHIEN.) Where are you going, darling? (*Crosses* U. S. C.)
BOIS D'ENG. I'm going to get dressed, darling. Wait for me. (*He exits* R.)
FIRMIN. (*He enters* U. S. L. *and crosses* C.) Madame! It's M'sieur Ignace de Fontanet. (*He exits* U. S. L., *closing the doors.*)
LUCETTE. I'd forgotten about him. (*She rises and crosses* D. S. R.) Lay another place . . .

NINI. (*She crosses to below table* L. *of* LUCETTE.)
Darling . . . You're not having *him* to lunch . . . ?

LUCETTE. Why not . . . ?

NINI. (*Without malice.*) His breath!

LUCETTE. (*Laughing.*) Well, it's not exactly Palma
Violets . . . but he wouldn't hurt a fly . . .

DE CHENNEV. (*Laughing.*) Depends how far away he
was when he said "hullo" to it . . . (*He crosses* D. L. *to
the* D. S. *corner of the sofa.*)

NINI. You're right!

(*Through the open hall door we can see* DE FONTANET
taking off his coat helped by FIRMIN. FIRMIN *then
enters* U. S. L.)

FIRMIN. M'sieur Ignace de Fontanet.

DE FONTANET. (*He enters and crosses below* FIRMIN *to*
U. S. *of* LUCETTE.) My sweetest songbird. Can I kiss your
little hand?

LUCETTE. Kiss Nini's. She was just talking about
you . . .

(DE FONTANET *crosses* R. *to* NINI.)

DE FONTANET. (*Bows, flattered, to* NINI.) You're too
kind! (*He crosses* L. *to* R. *of* DE CHENNEVIETTE. *To*
LUCETTE.) You were mad to ask me—you see—I always
accept your invitations!

LUCETTE. I really meant it . . .

DE FONTANET. (*Shaking* DE CHENNEVIETTE'S *hand,
speaks to* LUCETTE.) I hope you liked your wonderful review in the *Figaro?*

LUCETTE. (*She crosses to* R. *of* DE FONTANET, *leaving a
gap between them.*) I haven't read it . . .

DE FONTANET. (*Taking the* Figaro *out of his pocket.*)
Luckily I came provided with a copy . . .

LUCETTE. Let's see . . .

DE FONTANET. (*Unfolding the paper.*) Here it is . . .

(BOIS D'ENGHIEN *enters* R. *out of the bedroom.*)

BOIS D'ENG. There! I'm ready . . . (*Sees the newspaper.*) My God, another one! (*He throws himself between* LUCETTE *and* DE FONTANET *and snatches the paper.*) GIVE ME THAT!

EVERYONE. Not again!

(NINI *crosses* U. S. C.)

DE FONTANET. (*Astonished.*) What on earth's the matter?

BOIS D'ENG. Never read newspapers on an empty stomach. (*He rolls the newspaper into a ball.*)

LUCETTE. Oh please . . . It was my wonderful review!

BOIS D'ENG. (*Stuffing the paper into his pocket.*) I'll save it for you, darling! (*Aside.*) I'll tear the bloody thing up!

DE FONTANET. (*He crosses* R. *to* L. *of* BOIS D'ENGHIEN. *Challenging.*) M'sieur!

BOIS D'ENG. (*Challenging.*) M'sieur . . .

LUCETTE. (*She crosses to* L. *of* DE FONTANET.) It doesn't matter. (*Introducing them.*) M'sieur de Fontanet —one of my friends . . . M'sieur Bois d'Enghien. My *friend!*

DE FONTANET. (*Smiling.*) M'sieur . . .

BOIS D'ENG. (*Also smiling.*) M'sieur . . . (*They shake hands.*)

DE FONTANET. I must congratuate you, sir. On your excellent taste. I have long been a platonic lover of Madame Lucette Gautier in whom beauty and talent are so generously mixed. (*Looking at* BOIS D'ENGHIEN *who is gasping for breath.*) Aren't you feeling well?

(LUCETTE *crosses* U. S. *a little to try and distract* BOIS D'ENGHIEN'S *attention behind* DE FONTANET'S *back.* NINI *crosses to* U. S. R. *of* DE CHENNEVIETTE. *They try to conceal their giggles.*)

BOIS D'ENG. Do you notice a strange smell in here . . . ?

DE FONTANET. No . . . (*He sniffs.*)

BOIS D'ENG. (*Sniffs.*) Anyone trying to grow mushrooms in the basement?

DE FONTANET. Funny you should mention it . . .

BOIS D'ENG. Is it . . . ?

DE FONTANET. (*He crosses to* R. *of* NINI.) I can't think why it is. But people quite often ask me that.

LUCETTE. (*She crosses to* D. L. *of chair* L. *of table. Whispers to* BOIS D'ENGHIEN.) Darling . . . It's him!

BOIS D'ENG. Good heavens! That's what it is. (*Crossing* R. *to* DE FONTANET.) I'm terribly sorry . . . I had no idea . . .

DE FONTANET. (*Breathing at him.*) *What?*

BOIS D'ENG. (*Crosses to* L. *of* LUCETTE.) . . . Oh! Nothing . . . (*Aside.*) My God! He's not particularly fragrant. (*He moves* U. S.)

(LUCETTE *crosses to above table.*)

FIRMIN. (*Enters* U. S. R.) Lunch is served.

MARCELINE. (*Enters* U. S. R.) Women and children first! (*Exits* U. S. R.)

(BOIS D'ENGHIEN *laughs.*)

LUCETTE. (*Crosses* U. S. *to dining room below* BOIS D'ENGHIEN.) Come on, darlings, let's eat!

NINI. (*She crosses to* L. *of* LUCETTE *and kisses her.*) Goodbye, darling.

LUCETTE. Can't you really stay?

NINI. (*She crosses to* L. *of* BOIS D'ENGHIEN *and picks up her things from the sofa.*) No, really. Henri's taking me for a snack—at Cartiers!

(NINI *crosses to the* R. *of* DE FONTANET, *waving at him.*)

LUCETTE. (*While* NINI *is shaking hands with* DE

CHENNEVIETTE.) I hope when you're a Duchess you won't be too proud to call on me . . .

NINI. (*She crosses to L. of* LUCETTE.) Of course not! You'll be a nice change from all my respectable friends . . .

LUCETTE. (*Bowing.*) You're really living the part, aren't you, darling . . . ? (EVERYONE *laughs.*)

NINI. (*Taken aback, but laughing with the others.*) I didn't mean that . . . darling!

MARCELINE. (*Appearing at the dining room door with her mouth full.*) Are you all on a fast . . . ?

LUCETTE. Coming! (*Going with* NINI *to the hall.*) Goodbye, darling.

(NINI *crosses to* U. S. L. *door, followed by* LUCETTE *who remains in the doorway.*)

NINI. Bless you! And . . . take my advice. Don't let your Ferny off the lead again. (*Exits. Door slams off.*)

DE CHENNEV. (*Sitting on the piano stool.*) Nini Galant—married!

LUCETTE. (*Crosses D. S. to above sofa.*) Dear girl—she always wanted to go one better than her parents. (*Crosses to above* C. *chair.*) So let's go in to lunch . . . (BOIS D'ENGHIEN *goes into the dining room in front of her. To* DE FONTANET.) After you . . .

DE FONTANET. Excuse me . . .

(DE FONTANET *and* BOIS D'ENGHIEN *exit* U. S. R. *closing doors.*)

LUCETTE. (*To* DE CHENNEVIETTE.) Aren't you coming?

DE CHENNEV. (*Embarrassed.*) There's a little something . . . I hardly like to remind you.

LUCETTE. (*Crosses D. S. to R. of C. chair.*) A little what?

DE CHENNEV. Child.

LUCETTE. Whose child?

DE CHENNEV. Ours . . .

LUCETTE. Our little one . . . ! It can almost toddle . . .

DE CHENNEV. Yes! And it wants to toddle into the Bank and collect its monthly cheque.

LUCETTE. (*Crossing a little U. S. towards doors U. S. R.*) I'll give it you after lunch.

DE CHENNEV. (*Crosses below sofa to L. of LUCETTE.*) I hate to ask you. But really at his age he runs up the most enormous milk bills . . .

LUCETTE. It's not the milk bills I object to. It's his curious taste for cigars and vintage champagne . . .

DE CHENNEV. Doctor's orders—champagne brings up the wind!

FIRMIN. (*Enters through doors U. S. R.*) Mademoiselle Marceline wants to know if you're ever coming in to lunch.

LUCETTE. She'll have finished the oysters if we don't. Can't someone find that girl a lover?

(*The DOORBELL RINGS. FIRMIN crosses to U. S. L. doors.*)

FIRMIN. It never stops . . . (LUCETTE *and* DE CHENNEVIETTE *go into the dining room and are greeted with satisfied cries. The door shuts on them. FIRMIN lets the* BARONESS DUVERGER *into the room.*) I'm sorry, Madame. Madame's entertaining company at an informal luncheon . . . (FIRMIN *remains in the hall. The* BARONESS *crosses below him, and crosses* C.)

B. DUVERGER. Be good enough to announce me. I am the Baroness Duverger . . . On a vital matter. It can't be put off!

(FIRMIN *crosses to U. S. L. of the* BARONESS, *having closed the doors.*)

FIRMIN. I can but ask . . .

B. DUVERGER. Madame Gautier won't know me. Just

simply say . . . The Baroness Duverger wants to make use of her talents for a little family celebration.

(FIRMIN *shows the* BARONESS *to a chair* L. *of the table.*)

FIRMIN. I understand perfectly, Madame. (*The* BARONESS *sits. He crosses* U. S. *to the dining room. The BELL RINGS rings as he reaches the door. Smartly changing direction towards the* U. S. L. *doors.*) Excuse me! (*He exits through* U. S. L. *doors.*)

B. DUVERGER. (*Looks round her, takes out the* Figaro *she's brought with her, unfolds it. Pauses. Reads.*) "The Baroness Duverger is pleased to announce the forthcoming marriage of her daughter to M'sieur Bois d'Enghien." There it is. In black and white . . . (*Noises off. She goes on reading, nods her head with satisfaction.*) They said it would be in black and white . . .

(BOUZIN *enters in hall and crosses* C. *with* FIRMIN *backing in front of him.*)

BOUZIN. Please ask her to see me. Bouzin. My name's Bouzin. Can you possibly remember that? Do try . . .

FIRMIN. I might just manage it.

(FIRMIN *begins to cross* R., BOUZIN *pulls him back with his umbrella handle.*)

BOUZIN. Come on the matter of a song.

FIRMIN. A song?

BOUZIN. "Don't drop it on me doorstep" . . .

FIRMIN. Certainly not, M'sieur.

BOUZIN. Oh, that's the name of my song.

FIRMIN. Exceedingly quaint! Madame here is waiting . . .

BOUZIN. Oh . . . Thank you very much! (*He greets the* BARONESS *who raises her eyes for a moment in greeting.*)

FIRMIN. We've got more bells here than the Notre Dame!

(FIRMIN *exits* U. S. L. BOUZIN *crosses to put his umbrella on the piano stool, then moves slowly to the* R. *of the* BARONESS, *then to the doors* U. S. R. *and listens at the keyhole, then to the chair* C., *and sits. After a pause, he rises slowly and tries to see her newspaper, rising half off the chair.*)

BOUZIN. That's the *Figaro*, isn't it?

B. DUVERGER. (*Raising her head.*) Excuse me?

BOUZIN. (*Friendly.*) I said "Isn't that the *Figaro* you're reading?

B. DUVERGER. (*Surprised.*) Of course it's the *Figaro*. (*She goes on reading.*)

BOUZIN. (*Sits back in his chair.*) First class newspaper . . .

B. DUVERGER. (*Off-handed.*) Yes . . .

BOUZIN. Today's great news is on page four. You seen it . . . ?

B. DUVERGER. No . . .

BOUZIN. (*He rises and crosses to the* L. *of the* BARONESS *and takes her newspaper.*) No? Give it here. I'll show you. It's pretty sensational. (*He turns the pages.*) "Whispers from the Boulevards . . . at the Alcazar tiny, but talented Suzy Maya is having a great success with her new song "I thought he was a rotter . . . Until he cooked me a pig's trotter . . . And my heart just melted away . . ." (*He holds out the paper to the* BARONESS, *very satisfied.*) Read it for yourself!

B. DUVERGER. (*She takes the paper.*) Really, M'sieur! Why should I interest myself in a young woman . . . who's so utterly weak-minded as to change her opinions for the sake of a somewhat common dish . . . ?

BOUZIN. What . . . ?

B. DUVERGER. Isn't it a perfectly ludicrous situation?

BOUZIN. No.

B. DUVERGER. What?

BOUZIN. It's my song.

B. DUVERGER. You're a . . . literary man?

BOUZIN. A poet by vocation—a lawyer's clerk by force of circumstance. . . .

(FIRMIN *enters* U. S. L. *and crosses to the piano* D. S. *with a basket of flowers.*)

B. DUVERGER. ⎫
BOUZIN.   ⎬ Well . . . ?

(BOUZIN *crosses* U. S. L.)

FIRMIN. I have had no opportunity of speaking to Madame. Someone delivered this at the tradesman's entrance . . .

BOUZIN. Very sumptuous . . . Is it her birthday?

FIRMIN. Every day is a birthday for Lucette Gautier.

BOUZIN. Who sent them . . . ? Some demented millionaire?

FIRMIN. I couldn't say, M'sieur. There's no card. This particular tribute is from a gentleman who . . . (*He puts the flowers on the piano.*) prefers to remain anonymous.

BOUZIN. Wasting his money!

B. DUVERGER. Now, my good man, will you announce me?

FIRMIN. (*He crosses* U. S. R.) Without delay.

(BOUZIN *crosses* U. S. *to* L. *of* FIRMIN.)

BOUZIN. And you haven't forgotten my name?

FIRMIN. M'sieur Basin!

BOUZIN. No, Bouzin. B-O-U . . .

FIRMIN. Yes, of course.

BOUZIN. (*Putting his hat on the chair next to the sofa.*) Hang on, I'll give you a card . . . (*He looks for one of his cards.*)

FIRMIN. Please don't bother. I'll remember you by "Please don't drop it on me doorstep" . . . !

BOUZIN. Isn't it memorable! But in fact I have printed visiting cards . . . (FIRMIN *exits* U. S. R., *closing the doors in* BOUZIN'S *face as he follows him.* BOUZIN *moves back behind the sofa still searching for his card, and arrives at the piano.*) He'll get my name wrong, naturally. (*Looks at the bouquet.*) Exotic blooms! (*He's about to put away his pocket book, when he has an idea. Making sure that the* BARONESS *is still reading, he puts his card in the basket of flowers and moves* D. S.) If it's anonymous, it might as well do someone a favour. (*He puts his pocket book back in his pocket. Pause. Silence. He laughs. This makes the* BARONESS *raise her head.*) It really makes me laugh every time I think of that song. "Don't drop it on me doorstep . . ." (*Silence. The* BARONESS *starts to read again.* BOUZIN *laughs again, and crosses* C.) I expect you're dying to hear it, aren't you dear . . . ?

B. DUVERGER. I think I can contain my curiosity. (*She goes on reading.*)

BOUZIN. Oh, I don't mind. Everyone's always saying "Why don't you write a song for Lucette Gautier?" Of course she's just dying to do a Bouzin song . . . So . . . after a couple of sleepless years . . . I came up with this! (*The* BARONESS *puts down her newspaper. Sings.*)

> Me husband's been away
> For three years and a day
> And I've got a problem on me mind.
> When he comes home from sea
> I know he'll say to me
> "Don't drop the basket on me doorstep!"

(BOUZIN *dances to the* L. *of the* BARONESS *with his bowler hat under his jacket on the last line. He laughs, delighted.*) Did you understand it?

B. DUVERGER. Certainly not!

BOUZIN. (*Looks at her, and says suddenly.*) Of course

I recognize you . . . You're the stunning trapeze lady from the Eldorado! You're the one who swings from her toes in flesh-coloured tights waving a flag. I'm one of your greatest admirers!

B. DUVERGER. (*She rises.*) I'm afraid you're wrong. I'm the Baroness Duverger . . .

BOUZIN. Honestly? (*He bows.*) Well, cheer up, dear. At least you look like someone famous . . . (*He moves U. S. Noises off from the dining room. FIRMIN enters U. S. R. with a folded piece of paper. BOUZIN crosses to the L. of FIRMIN. Anxiously.*) Have you asked Madame Gautier about my song?

FIRMIN. I have, M'sieur.

BOUZIN. Enthusiastic, is she?

FIRMIN. Not exactly. She says it's a very stupid song, and to give it back to you at once.

BOUZIN. (*Drily.*) She says *what?*

FIRMIN. So here it is.

(FIRMIN *gives the song back to* BOUZIN *who crosses to the sofa and picks up his hat.*)

BOUZIN. I must say, I'm not surprised. It's rather above her usual level . . .

FIRMIN. (*Friendly.*) Listen to me, my friend! (FIRMIN *crosses D. S. to the R. of* BOUZIN.) Another time if you're thinking of working for Madame, kindly have a word with me first . . .

BOUZIN. (*Contemptuous.*) With you . . . ?

FIRMIN. With me! I have the ear of Madame.

BOUZIN. I wonder who's got the other one! (BOUZIN *crosses D. L. to the piano. Grumbling.*) Stupid! My song I worked on for two years . . . Stupid!

FIRMIN. Shall I see you out . . . ?

BOUZIN. (*Points to the basket of flowers.*) And after I . . . I've a good mind to . . . (*He picks up the basket as if he's going to take it away with him.*)

FIRMIN. Hey!

BOUZIN. No! At least I've got a generous nature . . . (*Puts the basket back on the piano.*) Goodbye.

(BOUZIN *bows and crosses* U. S. L. *and exits.*)

FIRMIN. (*Goes to shut the door.*) Goodbye to you. (*Door slams.*)

B. DUVERGER. What about me? Did you tell Madame . . . (*The* BARONESS *crosses* C.)

FIRMIN. Yes Madame; she's up to her eyes at the moment . . .

B. DUVERGER. Oh what a bore . . . !

FIRMIN. (*Crosses to the* L. *of the* BARONESS.) If Madame could call again . . . ?

B. DUVERGER. I suppose I'll have to. It's for an engagement party this evening. Will you tell Mademoiselle Gautier that I'll be back in an hour?

FIRMIN. Certainly, Madame. This way, Madame . . .

(FIRMIN *holds the door* U. S. L. *for the* BARONESS *to exit, then follows her out, shutting the doors. At the same moment,* DE CHENNEVIETTE *opens half of the* U. S. R. *doors and peers into the room. He enters and crosses* R., *then puts his coffee on the mantelpiece.*)

DE CHENNEV. The coast's clear.

EVERYONE. Good!

(DE FONTANET *enters and crosses* D. S. R.—*puts his coffee on the table.* BOIS D'ENGHIEN *enters also, crosses* L. *and sits on the sofa.* LUCETTE *enters and crosses* C.)

LUCETTE. (*To* BOIS D'ENGHIEN.) What's the matter, my beautiful one? You look a little sad.

BOIS D'ENG. Not at all. (*Aside.*) I've got to tell her now!

(LUCETTE *crosses above the sofa to behind* BOIS

D'ENGHIEN. *She throws her arms round his neck just as he is about to take a sip of coffee.*)

LUCETTE. Do you love me, darling?

BOIS D'ENG. Madly! (LUCETTE *crosses* U. S. C.) I've got a nasty feeling she's not going to take it like a man.

DE FONTANET. What gorgeous flowers!

EVERYONE. Where?

DE FONTANET. There!

EVERYONE. Oh . . . how gorgeous . . . !

(DE CHENNEVIETTE *crosses to the piano.*)

LUCETTE. Good heavens! Who can have sent them . . . ?

DE CHENNEV. (*Goes and takes the basket of flowers from the piano and comes* D. S. C.) Here's the card . . . (*Reads.*) Camille Bouzin . . . (*Crosses to* L. *of* LUCETTE.) Articled Clerk . . . Fancy that! (*He presents the basket to* LUCETTE.)

LUCETTE. Poor boy . . . I gave his song back and I wasn't very polite . . . (*She crosses* R. *to the mantelpiece.*) As a song writer, he's obviously a marvellous Articled Clerk. (*She smells the bouquet.*) They smell much too good for flowers . . . There's something in here . . .

EVERYONE. Oh!

(LUCETTE *takes a jewel case out of the flowers, and puts the basket on the mantelpiece.*)

DE CHENNEV. That's what she smelt . . . !

EVERYONE. A jewel case!

LUCETTE. A jewel case! (*She opens it and crosses* D. S. C.) No, it's too much . . . (*She takes out a ring and crosses to* L. *of table and sits.*)

BOIS D'ENG. What is . . . ?

(DE FONTANET *crosses to* U. S. R. *of* LUCETTE, DE

CHENNEVIETTE *to behind her and* BOIS D'ENGHIEN *crosses to her,* U. S. R.)

LUCETTE. Just rubies and diamonds, that's all. (*She puts the ring on her finger and shows them all.*)

EVERYONE. Oh . . . ! How beautiful!

LUCETTE. (*Trying to read the name on the jewel case.*) Cartier's naturally . . . It's really most peculiar. . . .

DE CHENNEV. He must be doing well. For an articled Clerk . . .

BOIS D'ENG. He must be . . . quite disgustingly rich . . .

DE FONTANET. I'd say—rich and madly in love!

LUCETTE. (*Laughing.*) Honestly?

(BOIS D'ENGHIEN *crosses* D. C.)

BOIS D'ENG. (*Aside.*) If I could only land this Bouzin fellow on her. Then I could creep out from underneath . . . I know I'm behaving like a bit of a cad . . .

(BOIS D'ENGHIEN *sits on* D. S. *end of the sofa.*)

LUCETTE. I suppose his song might have possibilities . . . all it needs is a writer.

DE CHENNEV. Like you, de Fontanet.

BOIS D'ENG. Like him!

(DE FONTANET *crosses to the* R. *of* BOIS D'ENGHIEN.)

DE FONTANET. Oh, you're too kind! I once wrote a song. It had a sort of catchword—I called it "Ah Futility!"

(EVERYONE *laughs.*)

BOIS D'ENG. People should be careful when they choose titles!

DE FONTANET. Did I say something funny . . . ?

(LUCETTE *rises and crosses* C. *to* R. *of* DE FONTANET.)

LUCETTE. . . . ~~No, it's Fernand. He's never serious!~~
(*Trying to change the subject and stop giggling.*) Do
come to the theatre tonight . . . ?
DE FONTANET. My dear Lady . . . I'm desolated. I'm
invited to an old friend, the Baroness Duverger's.

(LUCETTE *crosses to chair* L. *of table, and sits.*)

BOIS D'ENG. My future mother-in-law. (*He rises.*)
DE FONTANET. She's giving an engagement party. Her
daughter's going to marry a M'sieur . . . M'sieur . . .
I had it on the tip of my tongue . . .
BOIS D'ENG. (*Aside.*) Let's hope it drops off.
DE FONTANET. M'sieur . . . She did tell me.

(BOIS D'ENGHIEN *moves between* DE FONTANET *and*
LUCETTE.)

BOIS D'ENG. Who on earth cares what he's called?
DE FONTANET. Half a minute! I've got it! No . . . it's
a name like yours.

(BOIS D'ENGHIEN *crosses back* C.)

BOIS D'ENG. Impossible! There aren't any names like
mine!
LUCETTE. Why are you so nervous, darling?
BOIS D'ENG. I'm not in the least nervous! I just can't
stand it when people say "half a minute. I've got it . . .
it begins with Q . . ."
DE FONTANET. That's right—Q.
BOIS D'ENG. Potter!
DE FONTANET. No . . .
BOIS D'ENG. We're never going to meet him. Why
should we bother to find out his name?

(*There's a ring at the DOORBELL.*)

DE CHENNEV. As a matter of fact, he's right.

(BOIS D'ENGHIEN *takes* DE FONTANET D. L.)

BOIS D'ENG. So for God's sake, stop cudgelling your brains!

(FIRMIN *enters* U. S. L. *and crosses* C. *searching for something behind the furniture.*)

LUCETTE. What're you looking for, Firmin?
FIRMIN. Oh, nothing really. This Bouzin person alleges he forgot his umbrella . . .

(LUCETTE *crosses to the* R. *of* FIRMIN.)

EVERYONE. Bouzin!

(LUCETTE *crosses* U. S. C. *to* BOUZIN'S R. *as he enters* U. S. L.)

LUCETTE. But show him in!
EVERYONE. It's Bouzin!

(DE FONTANET *crosses to* DE CHENNEVIETTE *on his* R.)

LUCETTE. Do come in, M'sieur Bouzin. M'sieur Bouzin, meet my friends . . . (LUCETTE *brings* BOUZIN D. S.)
EVERYONE. (*Welcoming him.*) Hullo M'sieur Bouzin . . .

(FIRMIN *crosses to the table, takes a coffee cup and exits* U. S. R. BOIS D'ENGHIEN *closes the doors* U. S. L.)

BOUZIN. (*Amazed at the reception.*) I'm sorry. It's just that I'd forgotten my umbrella . . .
LUCETTE. Please M'sieur Bouzin! Do sit down . . .
(LUCETTE *takes chair* L. *of table and places it* D. S. C.)
EVERYONE. Please sit down, M'sieur Bouzin.

(BOIS D'ENGHIEN *takes chair* R. *of sofa and places it* D. S. C. L. LUCETTE *sits in* L. *chair,* BOUZIN *on the chair to her* R.)

BOUZIN. Really, you're too kind!

DE FONTANET. My honoured nightingale! I'll leave you . . . To discuss M'sieur Bouzin's art!

LUCETTE. You're going? I'll see you out . . .

(LUCETTE *rises and puts back her chair to* U. R. *of sofa.*)

DE FONTANET. Don't bother.

DE CHENNEV. I'd better go too. . . . I hate to remind you . . .

LUCETTE. Come too. I'll make out the little one's cheque at once.

DE CHENNEV. Ah! Excellent!

(LUCETTE *and* DE FONTANET *exit* U. S. L. *followed by* DE CHENNEVIETTE.)

LUCETTE. Excuse me, M'sieur Bouzin––I'll be back in a minute.

(BOUZIN *rises and replaces chair to* L. *of table.*)

BOIS D'ENG. (*Crosses* U. S. *and then to* BOUZIN *whom he seizes.*) All right, you! Yes or no. Are you in love with Lucette?

BOUZIN. Me?

BOIS D'ENG. Yes you! You can't hide these things. You're wildly, passionately in love with her. Courage! Your moment's come! Dive in!

BOUZIN. In? Where . . . ?

BOIS D'ENG. Be a man. Lucette's yours . . .

BOUZIN. But honestly . . .

BOIS D'ENG. Not a word to her today. But tomorrow

. . . attack at dawn. She'll drop into your lap like a ripe plum! (BOIS D'ENGHIEN *crosses* D. L. *The FRONT DOOR SLAMS.*)

BOUZIN. (*Aside.*) Funny man!

(LUCETTE *enters* U. S. L., *takes a chair from* U. R. *of sofa and places it on* L. *of* BOUZIN'S.)

LUCETTE. I'm sorry I abandoned you . . . Now we can talk without any interruptions . . .

BOUZIN. (*Aside.*) Actually, I like picking my own plums . . .

(LUCETTE *sits on her chair, followed by* BOUZIN *sitting on his* L. *of the table.*)

LUCETTE. I'm going to be cross with you, you naughty boy. Why did you take your lovely song away from us?

(BOIS D'ENGHIEN *crosses behind the table to chair* R.)

BOUZIN. Because your servant said you thought it was stupid.

LUCETTE. Your song stupid! He must have made a mistake . . .

BOIS D'ENG. (*Sits on chair* R. *of table.*) A mistake! That's what it was!

LUCETTE. And I also have to thank you for the beautiful flowers.

BOUZIN. Oh, please don't mention it . . .

LUCETTE. Why not mention it? It was a charming gesture.

BOIS D'ENG. Charming! Charming!

LUCETTE. (*Showing him the hand with the ring on it.*) And my ring? You've seen my ring . . . ?

BOUZIN. Your ring . . . ?

LUCETTE. You see . . . I'm wearing it already . . .

BOUZIN. So you are! (*Aside.*) What's her ring got to do with me?

LUCETTE. I must say . . . Your song's charming. There's no other word for it . . .

BOUZIN. You're too kind . . .

LUCETTE. Except for one thing . . .

BOUZIN. One thing . . . ?

LUCETTE. The words!

BOIS D'ENG. No. The words won't do.

BOUZIN. Is that all?

LUCETTE. Absolutely all. Except the tune!

BOIS D'ENG. The tune will have to go.

LUCETTE. You see, we do want to be constructive.

BOIS D'ENG. We feel it ought to have been written by someone else!

BOUZIN. Really? . . . But apart from that, you like it?

LUCETTE. } Enormously!
BOIS D'ENG.

BOIS D'ENG. I've got an idea! You could work on it together!

LUCETTE. We could work on it together. Now this is what we thought . . . Have you got your song on you?

BOUZIN. I left it at home . . .

LUCETTE. Oh dear!

BOUZIN. (*He rises.*) But I only live round the corner, in the Rue des Dames. I could run . . .

LUCETTE. (*She rises and puts her chair back* U. R. *of sofa.*) If it wouldn't be a bother . . .

BOUZIN. (*Crossing to* R. *of* LUCETTE.) It's the least I can do . . . I can easily make a few changes. I work very fast . . . sometimes . . .

BOIS D'ENG. Really?

BOUZIN. Sometimes a whole song'll just happen to me . . . Sometimes I can write one in five minutes . . .

BOIS D'ENG. (*Rising.*) You amaze me! (*Aside.*) Fancy being able to write anything as bad as that in five minutes . . .

(BOUZIN *crosses to doors* U. S. L., *below* LUCETTE.)

BOUZIN. I go . . .

LUCETTE. Your umbrella . . .

(BOUZIN *crosses* D. L. *to the piano for his umbrella.*)

BOUZIN. Oh yes. Of course. My umbrella. Like a flash of lightning! (*He exits through doors* U. S. L. LUCETTE *follows him out, closing the doors behind her.*)

(BOIS D'ENGHIEN *crosses to* C. *below chair* R. *of sofa.*)

BOIS D'ENG. Now for it! Courage! Blow the retreat and leave the field open for little Bouzin. All right then! A clean break . . .
LUCETTE. (*Offstage.*) It'll be lovely . . . Don't be long! (*The FRONT DOOR SLAMS.*)
BOIS D'ENG. (*Sits on the sofa.*) If only I knew how to begin: "Now look here, Lucette. . . ."

(LUCETTE *enters and crosses to behind* BOIS D'ENGHIEN *and puts her arms round his neck.*)

LUCETTE. What were you saying, darling?
BOIS D'ENG. I was saying "Now look here, Lucette."
LUCETTE. Do you really love me?
BOIS D'ENG. I was saying (*Weakly.*) "Now look here, Lucette—I really love you . . ." (*Aside.*) It's not going well . . .

(LUCETTE *crosses below the sofa.*)

LUCETTE. I know what he wants. Insatiable fellow . . . (*She sits on the* D. S. *end of the sofa.*) I was so happy when you came back last night. I really thought it was all over.
BOIS D'ENG. All over . . . ? Whatever gave you that idea?
LUCETTE. (*Delighted.*) And now I've *got* you for ever! (*Clasps* BOIS D'ENGHIEN *to her.*) Tell me I've got you.

BOIS D'ENG. (*Agreeing.*) Oh yes. You've got me!

LUCETTE. (*Looking into his eyes.*) For ever and ever . . .

BOIS D'ENG. (*Looking into her eyes.*) Endlessly . . .

(LUCETTE *pushes* BOIS D'ENGHIEN'S *face down and* D. S. *across her lap.*)

LUCETTE. Oh my Ferny . . . !

BOIS D'ENG. My Lu-Lu . . . ! (LUCETTE *is now lying with* BOIS D'ENGHIEN *in a very uncomfortable position. Aside.*) What a terrible way to break off a romance!

LUCETTE. (*Langourously.*) Comfy, darling . . . ?

BOIS D'ENG. Mmm. (*Aside, agonised.*) I think she's broken my spine . . .

LUCETTE. I'd like to just lie like this . . . for the next twenty years. Wouldn't you . . . ?

BOIS D'ENG. Well, twenty years is a long time . . .

LUCETTE. (*Stroking his back.*) I'd say . . . "My Ferny" and you'd answer "My Lu-Lu." And the years'd just roll by.

(BOIS D'ENGHIEN *returns to a sitting position.*)

BOIS D'ENG. (*Aside.*) Never a dull moment!

LUCETTE. (*Rises and crosses* C.) Come on then, impatient fellow . . .

BOIS D'ENG. (*Aside.*) I know what's coming . . .

LUCETTE. Come with me and hook up my dress, darling . . .

BOIS D'ENG. (*Sulky.*) Not again!

LUCETTE. (*Moves* D. S.) What's the matter?

BOIS D'ENG. (*Rises and takes his courage in both hands.*) I've got to tell you! We can't go on like this!

LUCETTE. Like what?

BOIS D'ENG. Like this! (*Takes one pace* D. S. *Aside.*) Now . . . Here we go . . . (*To* LUCETTE.) The day's got to come when I have to take a deep breath and say . . . "Lucette!"

LUCETTE. (*Takes one pace* D. L. *to* BOIS D'ENGHIEN.)
Yes darling?

BOIS D'ENG. "Lucette, we must part . . ."

(LUCETTE *moves* D. L., *nearer to* BOIS D'ENGHIEN.)

LUCETTE. (*Astonished.*) What?

BOIS D'ENG. Yes, we must. (*Aside.*) Now . . . light the
blue touch paper and stand well clear.

(LUCETTE *turns* R. *away from* BOIS D'ENGHIEN *and moves*
away R. *from him.*)

LUCETTE. (*Seeing the light.*) You're going to get
married . . .

BOIS D'ENG. Me? (*His courage failing.*) Whoever gave
you that idea?

LUCETTE. You did!

BOIS D'ENG. It's not like that . . . It's . . . my finan-
cial position. I can't give you the bare minimum of
luxuries you need to exist and . . .

LUCETTE. Oh, is that all! (*She laughs and crosses* L.
to embrace him.) Silly boy! (*She releases him and sighs*
passionately.) Isn't my love enough for you . . . ?

BOIS D'ENG. (*Aside.*) Enough? It's too much.

(LUCETTE *crosses* R. C.)

LUCETTE. (*Aside.*) He's up to something. I don't know
what it is . . . (*To* BOIS D'ENGHIEN.) What a horrible
moment—when I thought you were going to get married.
(*She turns to* BOIS D'ENGHIEN.) Swear to me you'll never
get married! Swear! (*She moves back to him and holds*
on to him as if she were about to lose him.)

BOIS D'ENG. Swear?

LUCETTE. Swear!

BOIS D'ENG. I swear!

(LUCETTE *crosses* R. *to chair above table.*)

LUCETTE. Thanks! If you ever got married—I promise you . . . I'll know exactly what to do.

BOIS D'ENG. (*Worried.*) What exactly . . . ?

LUCETTE. (*Sits on the chair.*) It'd be over quickly. One neat little bullet through the head.

BOIS D'ENG. (*Eyes popping.*) Through whose head?

LUCETTE. Mine of course.

BOIS D'ENG. (*Relieved.*) That's not so bad . . .

(LUCETTE *nervously picks up the* Figaro *that the* BARONESS *left behind.*)

LUCETTE. I'm not afraid to die. If ever I picked up the *Figaro* and read in the engagement column . . .

BOIS D'ENG. (*Aside, too terrified to move.*) My God! She's just going to!

LUCETTE. I'm being stupid. It's never going to happen . . . Why should I even think about it?

(LUCETTE *throws the* Figaro *down on the table.* BOIS D'ENGHIEN *crosses* R. *to above table and leaps on the* Figaro *and stuffs it under his jacket.*)

BOIS D'ENG. (*Aside.*) The place is crawling with *Figaros!* They must come here to breed . . .

(LUCETTE *turns to him at the noise he makes. He laughs weakly and she throws herself in his arms.*)

LUCETTE. And you'll love me for ever and ever?

BOIS D'ENG. For ever and ever!

LUCETTE. My darling!

BOIS D'ENG. (*Aside.*) Until next week . . .

(BOIS D'ENGHIEN *sits on the chair* L. *of the table.* DE CHENNEVIETTE *enters* U. S. L. *closing the doors and crosses* D. C. *with an envelope.*)

DE CHENNEV. 5,000 francs! I'm registering this letter. Have you got a 40 centimes stamp?

LUCETTE. (*Crossing* R. *to her bedroom.*) Yes, in there. Wait.

DE CHENNEV. Let me owe you the money.

LUCETTE. I don't need your money.

DE CHENNEV. I must pay my wack!

LUCETTE. Don't be silly. (*She exits.*)

DE CHENNEV. (*Crossing to the sofa. He sits in the centre of it.*) It's strange. Women have no sense of honour about this sort of thing. What's the matter with you, old chap? You look miserable . . .

BOIS D'ENG. Not at all. I'm bloody desperate.

DE CHENNEV. It sounds bad!

(BOIS D'ENGHIEN *rises, crosses to the chair* R. *of the sofa and sits.*)

BOIS D'ENG. There's something . . . I can't tell Lucette. But, I mean, well you're almost her husband. You've got to part us.

DE CHENNEV. If I were Lucette's husband . . . I wouldn't think of parting her from her lover!

BOIS D'ENG. You must!

DE CHENNEV. Whatever for?

BOIS D'ENG. The truth is, I'm on the point of getting married . . .

DE CHENNEV. You!

BOIS D'ENG. Me. The engagement party's tonight!

DE CHENNEV. Good Lord! Lucette won't like that.

BOIS D'ENG. (*Takes* DE CHENNEVIETTE's *arm possessively.*) But . . . it's . . . for her own good. She must end our affair at once . . .

DE CHENNEV. Well. (*Thoughtfully.*) If she wants an excuse, you getting married *might* do . . .

(*The BELL RINGS.*)

BOIS D'ENG. Tell her that! For God's sake have a serious talk with her. She'll listen to you . . .

DE CHENNEV. Don't you believe it . . .

(FIRMIN *enters through doors* U. S. L. *and crosses* C.)

FIRMIN. M'sieur the General Irrigua.

DE CHENNEV. Ah good. Show him in. (FIRMIN *starts to go.*) No. Wait till we're gone. (DE CHENNEVIETTE *and* BOIS D'ENGHIEN *rise,* DE CHENNEVIETTE *goes* U. S. R. C. *and* BOIS D'ENGHIEN *to his right. To* BOIS D'ENGHIEN.) Come on! This way out.

(FIRMIN *exits* U. S. L.)

BOIS D'ENG. Why?

DE CHENNEV. We'd only be in the way—the General . . .

BOIS D'ENG. You mean the millionaire who sees her show six times a week?

DE CHENNEV. Exactly! He's your only hope . . .

(DE CHENNEVIETTE, *followed by* BOIS D'ENGHIEN, *exits through doors* U. S. R.)

BOIS D'ENG. Power to his elbow! Lead on!

DE CHENNEV. This way.

(FIRMIN *enters through doors* U. S. L. MARCELINE *enters through doors* D. S. L. *at the moment that* FIRMIN *is going to let in the* GENERAL.)

MARCELINE. Who rang, Firmin?

FIRMIN. The General Irrigua, Mademoiselle.

MARCELINE. The General! Quick let him in, and then go and warn my sister . . . !

(MARCELINE *crosses* D. S. *in front of the piano.*)

FIRMIN. If M'sieur would step this way . . .

(*The* GENERAL *enters* U. S. L. *and crosses* D. S. L. C.)

GENERAL. Bueno! I am stepped already . . .

(*The* GENERAL *comes in. A large man with a strong Mexican/Spanish accent. He is followed by* ANTONIO *who enters* U. S. L. *and crosses* C. *He is carrying a large bouquet in front of him, and a small bouquet behind his back. He, in turn, is followed by* FIRMIN *who looks at him.*)

MARCELINE. (*Curtsies.*) General!
GENERAL. The little sister. How you? Camarero! Camarero! (*He turns to* FIRMIN.) Chamber man!
FIRMIN. (*Moves down.*) You talking to me?
GENERAL. Of course I'm talking to you . . . (*He crosses to* FIRMIN *and gives him his hat and cane.*) I'm not talking to me. (*Aside.*) Gringo! (*Aloud.*) You can tell the Mistress that I am stepped in!
FIRMIN. Yes, General. (*Aside as he goes to the* L. *of the room.*) He's a general nuisance that one . . . (*To* LUCETTE *as she comes out of her room.*) The Fleet's in . . . Madame.

(LUCETTE *enters* R. *and crosses* D. R. *to* D. R. *of table.* FIRMIN *crosses to doors* U. S. R., *exits and closes the doors.*)

GENERAL. (*To* LUCETTE *who is astonished to see him.*) Ah. The Mistress. At last we meet in person. This is my most gorgeous hour . . .

(LUCETTE *still looks astonished.* MARCELINE *introduces her to the* GENERAL.)

MARCELINE. This is General Irrigua, Lucette . . .
GENERAL. (*Bowing.*) El Estupendo!

(LUCETTE *crosses to the* R. *of the* GENERAL *and gives him her hand.*)

LUCETTE. Oh, General . . . I'm so sorry . . . (*Greeting* ANTONIO.) M'sieur . . . ?

GENERAL. De nada. That my interpreter . . . Antonio . . . The flowery tributes! (ANTONIO *crosses to the* L. *of the* GENERAL, *his hands behind his back, gives a large bouquet to the* GENERAL *who gives it to* LUCETTE. ANTONIO *steps back* U. S.) Uno, dos, tres!

LUCETTE. They're ravishing!

GENERAL. No! The ravishing is for me to do, Madame. If you please. And now . . . I have not forgotten the lil sister.

(*The* GENERAL *crosses* L. *to* MARCELINE, *taking the small bouquet from* ANTONIO *and giving it to* MAR-CELINE.)

MARCELINE. (*Taking the bouquet.*) Really! For me?

GENERAL. A little cheaper than the other but more easy to carry. (*To* ANTONIO.) You go and waiting for me in the halls!

ANTONIO. Yes, my General!

(*Exit* ANTONIO U. S. L. *closing the doors.*)

LUCETTE. (*Crossing* L. *towards the* GENERAL.) Sweet of you! I adore flowers . . .

GENERAL. (*Moving towards* LUCETTE.) I am very sweet.

MARCELINE. (*Smelling her tiny bouquet.*) I adore them too . . .

GENERAL. (*Over his shoulder.*) All right. But I am only sweet for Madame. Not for the whole familias.

LUCETTE. (*Untying the bouquet and crossing below the* GENERAL *to the* R. *of* MARCELINE.) Look, Marceline. Aren't they beautiful!

GENERAL. I have for you executed the rose bush!

LUCETTE. Executed!

GENERAL. Cut off all the heads!

LUCETTE. You're romantic!
MARCELINE. Oh, yes!

(MARCELINE *puts her head over* LUCETTE'S *shoulder.*)

GENERAL. Ethepthionally!
LUCETTE. And you're so clever at talking . . .

(LUCETTE *crosses below the* GENERAL *and puts the flowers in the vase on the mantelpiece* R. *The* GENERAL *does bull fighting movements as she passes him.*)

MARCELINE. I should think you have to be with an accent like that . . .
LUCETTE. (*To* MARCELINE.) Leave us alone, darling.
MARCELINE. Me?
GENERAL. (*Grandly.*) Leave us alone, the lil sister!
MARCELINE. Very well!
GENERAL. (*With great courtesy.*) Please! Do us such a favour, Mademoiselle . . . GET OUT!
MARCELINE. Very well! (MARCELINE *crosses to the door* D. L., *and turns to* LUCETTE.) The man's uncivilized!

(MARCELINE *exits through doors* D. L. *The* GENERAL *crosses below table to* L. *of* LUCETTE.)

GENERAL. (*Sharply.*) You! Yes, you there! Now I am near you. I breathe you in at last. We are alone . . .
LUCETTE. Please, do sit down . . .

(LUCETTE *sits on the chair* L. *of the table.*)

GENERAL. (*Passionately.*) I can't sit down . . . (*He crosses* L. C. *then* U. C. *to* C.)
LUCETTE. Why ever not . . . ?
GENERAL. I am too much in love! When I got your letter: that we might meet . . . (*He crosses to* L. *of* LUCETTE.) Caramba! Caramba!

LUCETTE. Are you feeling quite well?

GENERAL. Not at all. I am sweat in perthpirathions! Lucette! I am your lover . . . ! (*He tries to kiss the back of* LUCETTE's *neck.* LUCETTE *rises and moves* R. *below the table to above the chair to the* R. *of it.*)

LUCETTE. Careful, General. You're treading dangerous ground.

GENERAL. (*Crossing* L. C.) I'm used to danger! In my country I was Minister of War!

LUCETTE. You . . . ?

GENERAL. (*Bows.*) El Estupendo!

(LUCETTE *crosses to the* R. *of the* GENERAL.)

LUCETTE. What an honour! The first time I've been approached by a Member of the Cabinet . . .

GENERAL. Esss . . . !

LUCETTE. You don't sound *well* . . .

GENERAL. I am Esss . . .

LUCETTE. I really think you should sit down. (*Aside.*) He sounds like a gas leak . . .

GENERAL. Esss-Minister of War. Not any more . . .

LUCETTE. What are you now?

GENERAL. I am condemned to the death. La Muerte! By shooting.

LUCETTE. (*Startled.*) Really?

GENERAL. I was bringing to your country for a mission on my government. I am buying for my peoples, naval matters . . .

LUCETTE. (*Puzzled.*) Naval matters . . . ?

GENERAL. Twelve battleships.

LUCETTE. (*Not following.*) Well . . .

GENERAL. I loose them.

LUCETTE. Remarkably careless.

GENERAL. At roulette.

LUCETTE. At roulette?

GENERAL. In the Casino. At La Touquette.

LUCETTE. (*Crossing below table* R.) Hard luck!

GENERAL. That's enough about me! I have come to place myself at your disposal!

LUCETTE. At my what?

GENERAL. Disposal of me!

LUCETTE. Why?

(*The* GENERAL *crosses to the* L. *of* LUCETTE.)

GENERAL. Because I am so crazy, mad about you, Lucette! Your skin, your hair, your smells, your face, your eyes . . . You have absolutamente . . . (*His voice changes.*) Excuse me a moment . . . (*The* GENERAL *crosses* U S. *to doors,* U. S. L.) Antonio!

(ANTONIO *appears at the hall doors, and takes a few paces to* U. C.)

ANTONIO. Here my General!

GENERAL. How I say "subjugar"?

ANTONIO. Sub-ju-gate.

GENERAL. (*Dismissing him.*) Bueno! Gracias, Antonio!

ANTONIO. Gracias!

(ANTONIO *exits* U. S. L., *closing the doors. The* GENERAL *crosses to* L. *of* LUCETTE.)

GENERAL. (*Suddenly back in the passionate voice.*) You have subjugate me—so all I have is yours. My life . . . my money . . . Down to the last dollar. I will stripping naked for you.

LUCETTE. That won't be necessary!

GENERAL. I am struggling in poverty!

(LUCETTE *crosses* D. S.)

LUCETTE. Do you know what poverty is?

(GENERAL *crosses* L. C. *and turns* U. L. C.)

GENERAL. Oh excuse me, yes! Before I joined the Army as a humble General I was a humble school teacher. I used to teach your beautiful language.

(LUCETTE *crosses* L. *to below chair* L. *of table, and tries not to laugh.*)

LUCETTE. You mean you can speak it . . . ?

(*The* GENERAL *crosses to* LUCETTE, *then back* D. C.)

GENERAL. In my own country I speak it beautiful. But as soon as I get here I speak it very bad.

LUCETTE. (*Laughing.*) I do understand. (*She points to the sofa, and sits down on the chair* L. *of the table.*) Please . . . sit down.

GENERAL. (*Excited.*) I can't. Before you I can only sit down on my knees! (*He kneels and kisses* LUCETTE'S *foot.*) You're the goddess I kneel before. You are the pure virginal Santos!

LUCETTE. You're exaggerating!

GENERAL. (*Businesslike.*) Where your bedroom?

LUCETTE. (*Taken aback.*) What?

GENERAL. (*Passionately.*) I say again—where your bedroom?

(LUCETTE *rises.*)

LUCETTE. (*Aside.*) He said it again.

(*The* GENERAL *pulls* LUCETTE *down again.*)

GENERAL. It is love speaking through my voice! Because I want you! I must have you! It is necessary I live with you! And because the bedroom of the lady I adore is . . . (*Gets up.*) Excuse me a moment . . . (*The* GENERAL *crosses to the doors* U. S. L. ANTONIO *appears at the doors.*)

LUCETTE. (*Aside.*) Thank God that's over!

GENERAL. (*At the hall doors.*) Antonio! (*The GENERAL crosses* C. *followed by* ANTONIO.)

ANTONIO. Here my General!

GENERAL. Tabernaculo?

ANTONIO. Oh yes?

GENERAL. How I say it?

ANTONIO. Tabernacle!

GENERAL. Bueno! Gracias, Antonio.

ANTONIO. Bueno!

(ANTONIO *exits* U. S. L. *The* GENERAL *crosses back to* LUCETTE *in a businesslike way and kneels in front of her as before. Pauses a moment and then bursts out.*)

GENERAL. The bedroom is the holy tabernacle of the goddess you love! Holy Ground! Not to be stepid on!

(*The* GENERAL *is holding her hand, her left hand. She puts her right hand—with the ring on it—on his.*)

LUCETTE. . . . Let's leave it like that, shall we?

GENERAL. (*Looking at the ring.*) Just a moment. I think you have a ring on your finger . . .

LUCETTE. A ring. Oh yes . . . you noticed that . . .

GENERAL. A pretty thing, isn't it?

(LUCETTE *rises and goes* D. S.)

LUCETTE. It's just a trinket.

(*The* GENERAL *rises.*)

GENERAL. A trink . . . what?

LUCETTE. A mere bagatelle . . .

GENERAL. A bacatil? Excuse me a moment. (*The* GENERAL *crosses to the doors* U. S. L. *Calling.*) Antonio!

ANTONIO. (*Appears as before.*) My General!

GENERAL. What a "bacatil"? In Spanish? (*The* GEN-
ERAL *crosses* C. *followed by* ANTONIO.)

ANTONIO. "Bacatil"? Never heard of it.

LUCETTE. I told him it's a bagatelle.

ANTONIO. Oh, bagatelle! La senero dice usted que es
. . . poca cosa.

GENERAL. Oh yes of course. Bacatil . . . (*Dismissing*
ANTONIO.) Bueno! Bueno! Gracias Antonio.

ANTONIO. Bueno! (ANTONIO *exits* U. S. L.)

GENERAL. A bacatil. Yes of course.

LUCETTE. (*Crossing to below table.*) I keep it . . . for
purely sentimental reasons.

GENERAL. (*Moved.*) So brave of you—mia amada.

LUCETTE. It belonged to my dear, dead mother.

GENERAL. (*Astonished.*) Strange—the dead mother.

LUCETTE. Why, General?

GENERAL. Because I send the dear, dead Mother's ring
this morning to you . . . in a bouquette.

LUCETTE. You!

GENERAL. El Estupendo!

LUCETTE. It was him? You? Really *you?* (*She crosses
to* L. *below sofa, then back* C., *then crosses to above chair*
R. *of sofa, then behind sofa to in front of* D. S. *end of it.*)
Him?

GENERAL. I have spoken it!

LUCETTE. (*Aside.*) Oh, it's too much. That Bouzin.
Borrowing other peoples' presents. Pretending to qualify
as a lover. That sheep in wolf's clothing! (*She arrives at
the doors* U. S. L.)

ANTONIO. Bueno!

LUCETTE. Bueno!

GENERAL. What's the matter?

(LUCETTE *crosses* D. L.)

LUCETTE. Oh, nothing . . .

GENERAL. (*Teasing her.*) Still surprised to get the dead
Mother's ring . . . ?

LUCETTE. My Mothers . . . ? Oh, that's another one
. . . of course. Yes. I didn't know . . . or I should've
said thank you!

(*The* GENERAL *crosses to the* R. *of* LUCETTE *and kisses her
     hand.*)

GENERAL. Don't mention it. A mere bacatil. This goes
with this. (*The* GENERAL *crosses* D. C. *and brings out another jewel case.*) A bacatil bracelet . . .

(LUCETTE *crosses to* L. *of the* GENERAL.)

LUCETTE. (*Taking the case.*) What've I done to de-
serve . . . ?
GENERAL. (*Simply.*) You are loved. By me!

(*The* GENERAL *throws the case over his shoulder, and
     puts the bracelet on* LUCETTE'S *wrist.*)

LUCETTE. You love me? But why . . . ?
GENERAL. Because I do.
LUCETTE. Don't say it!
GENERAL. (*Determined.*) I do say it!
LUCETTE. No . . . Don't . . .
GENERAL. I do!

(LUCETTE *holds out the wrist with the bracelet on it.*)

LUCETTE. Then you must take back your presents . . .
GENERAL. Why?
LUCETTE. Because I can't ever love you! Not possi-
bly . . .
GENERAL. (*Surprised.*) Not possible? I am lovely . . .
LUCETTE. Yes, I know. But my special lover's back.
GENERAL. Your lover! Is he a *man* . . . ?
LUCETTE. Naturally!

(*The* GENERAL *crosses below* LUCETTE *to below the sofa.*)

GENERAL. Caramba! Hombre! A *man*. I comprende. He is a *man!*

LUCETTE. Please . . . Keep calm . . .

(*The* GENERAL *crosses* U. S. *to* C.)

GENERAL. (*In despair.*) I've heard something. There is a man passioning with you . . . A pretty man!

LUCETTE. Very pretty!

(*The* GENERAL *crosses* D. L. *to below sofa.*)

GENERAL. My God! He creeps upon the world. Who is this man?

(LUCETTE *crosses to* R. *of the* GENERAL.)

LUCETTE. Look. Please . . . General.

GENERAL. (*Purple with rage.*) What is he?

LUCETTE. (*Putting her hands gently on his shoulders.*) Cheer up. If I were free, I'd rather have you than anyone else.

GENERAL. To be your lover?

LUCETTE. (*Looking at the bracelet on her wrist.*) You seem to have excellent qualifications . . .

GENERAL. But . . .

LUCETTE. But I'm not free!

GENERAL. (*Continued despair.*) Lucette! You have smashed to pieces my heart.

(LUCETTE *crosses* R. *to* D. C.)

LUCETTE. What can I do? You see . . . whilst I'm in love with him I really can't love anyone else.

GENERAL. (*After a struggle, resigned.*) Bueno! (GENERAL *crosses to* L. *of* LUCETTE.) How many days will it take you?

LUCETTE. What?

GENERAL To be in love with *him?*

LUCETTE. Oh, just as long as he lives.

GENERAL. As long as he is living—eh! Ah-ha! (*The* GENERAL *crosses* L.) That should not take long . . .

LUCETTE. (*Aside.*) What's he talking about exactly?

(*The* GENERAL *crosses* U. L. *to behind* U. S. *end of the sofa.*)

GENERAL. Never you trouble the pretty head.

LUCETTE. (*Aside.*) This fellow can be exceedingly creepy! (*There's a knock at the dining room doors.*) Come in. Who is it?

BOIS D'ENG. (*Half opening the door and disguising his voice.*) Someone wants to see Madame Gautier . . .

(LUCETTE *recognises his voice and crosses* U. S. R., *the* GENERAL *following.*)

LUCETTE. All right. I'm coming.

(*She opens the door. The* GENERAL *pulls it wide open violently, with* BOIS D'ENGHIEN *still hanging on to the door knob on the other side. He pulls* BOIS D'ENGHIEN *to* C., *on his* R., *and* LUCETTE *crosses to* BOIS D'ENGHIEN'S R.)

GENERAL. You! What think you do?

LUCETTE. This is M'sieur Bois d'Enghien, General. An old friend—*nothing more.*

BOIS D'ENG. An old friend! That's exactly it. Absolutely nothing more!

GENERAL. (*Suspicious.*) An old friend, eh? And nothing more?

LUCETTE. Absolutely nothing more!

BOIS D'ENG. In fact rather less.

GENERAL. Bueno! If this is amigo—old friend . . .

(*The* GENERAL *shakes* BOIS D'ENGHIEN'S *hand.* FIRMIN *enters* U. S. L. *and crosses to* R. *of* LUCETTE.)

FIRMIN. Madame?

LUCETTE. Yes?

FIRMIN. It's the lady who came about your singing at an engagement party. I put her in the dining room . . .

LUCETTE. All right. I'm coming. (FIRMIN *goes out through the hall doors, leaving them wide open.*) Excuse me a moment, General.

GENERAL. I excuse . . .

(*The* GENERAL *crosses* L. *to behind sofa.*)

BOIS D'ENG. (*Aside to* LUCETTE.) That's lovely! What do I do now?

LUCETTE. Have a nice chat with the General . . . Try not to upset him . . .

BOIS D'ENG. All right. But don't be long.

LUCETTE. Of course I won't, darling.

(LUCETTE *exits* U. S. R. *Pause. The* GENERAL *and* BOIS D'ENGHIEN *exchange nervous smiles—and can't think of anything to say.*)

GENERAL. (*Breaking the silence.*) Always on the moving about—not me, Mamselle Gautier.

BOIS D'ENG. I should say so!

(*Pause. The* GENERAL *crosses below the sofa to the* L. *of* BOIS D'ENGHIEN.)

GENERAL. You are a piece of the music hall actings with her?

BOIS D'ENG. What am I?

GENERAL. As you are a friend then I suppose you are a piece of her actings . . .

BOIS D'ENG. Am I? Oh yes. Part of the act . . . Yes, of course. That's exactly what I am! (*He takes one pace* D. S. *Aside.*) Why do I say things like that? (*The* GENERAL *follows him.*)

GENERAL. Comprende . . . You are the tenor voice.

BOIS D'ENG. How did you guess? (*He takes a pace* D. S., *followed by the* GENERAL. *Aside.*) And I've got absolutely no ear for music . . .

GENERAL. I tell by the bumps!

BOIS D'ENG. The what?

GENERAL. A bumps reader! And bad at it! (*The* GENERAL *signals to* BOIS D'ENGHIEN *to sing.*)

BOIS D'ENG. (*Sings tunelessly.*) They call me Mimi!

(*The* GENERAL *crosses* L., *pulls a face, spits.*)

GENERAL. (*Aside.*) Nombre de dios! Horrifico voice!

BOIS D'ENG. (*Coughing badly.*) Lot of laryngitis about this year . . .

GENERAL. And tell me this, Bodyguard . . .

(BOIS D'ENGHIEN *crosses to the* R. *of the* GENERAL.)

BOIS D'ENG. Pardon me. *Bois d'Enghien!*

GENERAL. That's what I say—"Bodyguard."

BOIS D'ENG. Have it your own way . . .

GENERAL. (*Putting his arm in* BOIS D'ENGHIEN'S—*very confidential.*) You know Mamselle Gautier very well indeed?

BOIS D'ENG. We've kept in touch with each other over the years . . .

GENERAL. Is there . . . please. A lover?

BOIS D'ENG. What . . . ?

GENERAL. (*Letting go his arm.*) Calma! Calma! She told me . . .

BOIS D'ENG. Oh, did she? (*He crosses* R. *Aside.*) I needn't have sung at all . . .

GENERAL. Is he a very pretty fellow?

BOIS D'ENG. That's hardly for me to say . . .

GENERAL. (*Puzzled.*) But there seem to be no pretty men about here.

BOIS D'ENG. (*Aside.*) Speak for yourself . . .

GENERAL. Bueno! As you know this man so well. *Who he?*

BOIS D'ENG. (*Aside.*) What've I got to lose? (BOIS D'ENGHIEN *crosses to the* L. *to the* GENERAL'S R.) You really want to know . . . who he?

GENERAL. Si! who he?

BOIS D'ENG. Oh, all right . . . (*He laughs.*) Shall I tell you?

GENERAL. Al instanto! (*Savagely.*) So I can kill him . . .

BOIS D'ENG. (*Crossing* R., *aside.*) I think he means it. (*Turns to the* GENERAL, *laughing.*) Very good joke! Yes, very funny. Absolutely . . . killing.

(*The* GENERAL *laughs with him. They're both on the* L. *and as this is going on, through the open door to the hall the* BARONESS *crosses from the dining room, through the hall and off.* LUCETTE *stops in the* U. S. L. *doors. The* GENERAL *crosses to the* L. *of* BOIS D'ENGHIEN.)

LUCETTE. (*When the* BARONESS *is out of sight.*) Very well, Madame. This evening then . . . That will be perfect.

(*The DOOR SLAMS.*)

GENERAL. Was *that . . . ?*

BOIS D'ENG. (*Seeing* LUCETTE.) Ssh . . . later.

GENERAL. (*Crossing* L. *to below the sofa.*) Oh bueno! Bueno!

BOIS D'ENG. (*Aside.*) Kill me! Charming fellow!

(BOIS D'ENGHIEN *crosses to* U. R. *of table.* LUCETTE *enters* U. S. L. *and crosses to* L. *of* BOIS D'ENGHIEN. *She is carrying an invitation card.*)

LUCETTE. I'm going to sing at a party tonight . . . (*To the* GENERAL.) Excuse me a moment, General.

GENERAL. I excuse!

LUCETTE. (*About to go into her room, moves towards* BOIS D'ENGHIEN.) I'm going to a party tonight. Won't you come with me? I can ask anyone I like . . .

BOIS D'ENG. I really can't tonight, darling. (LUCETTE *crosses to* L. *of the* GENERAL *who moves towards her. Aside.*) *I'm* going to a party tonight.

LUCETTE. What about you, General?

GENERAL. I am delight!

LUCETTE. I'll look forward to seeing you there, then. Here's the invitation. (*She gives a card to the* GENERAL.)

GENERAL. Muchas gracias! (*He kisses* LUCETTE'S *hand. The* GENERAL *puts the invitation card into his pocket.*)

LUCETTE. I'll be back soon.

(LUCETTE *exits into bedroom* U. R. *The* GENERAL *crosses* R. *to chair* L. *of table.*)

GENERAL. Well. What's she called?

(BOIS D'ENGHIEN *sits on the chair* R. *of table.*)

BOIS D'ENG. Who's she?

GENERAL. She's the man.

BOIS D'ENG. Which man is she?

GENERAL. She, the lover man!

BOIS D'ENG. (*Toying with the ring box that's been left on the table.*) Oh she's . . . he's called (*Sudden inspiration.*) Bouzin!

(*The* GENERAL *rises and crosses* L. *to behind* D. S. *end of sofa.*)

GENERAL. Poussin? All right . . . Morir! Morir Poussin! Stuck in the guts, Poussin!

(*The DOORBELL RINGS.* FIRMIN *appears in the* U. S. L. *doorway.*)

Bois d'Eng. (*Aside.*) Very depressing company, this fellow!

(Firmin *appears in the* u. s. l. *doorway.*)

Firmin. M'sieur Bouzin!
General. *Who?*

(Bois d'Enghien *rises.*)

Bois d'Eng. Oh God . . . it's him!

(Bouzin *enters very cheerfully and puts his umbrella by the chair by the sofa. He crosses to* l. *of* Bois d'Enghien, *the* General *crosses* r. *towards* Bouzin.)

Bouzin. I've got the song . . . Where's Lucette Gautier?
Bois d'Eng. (*Seeing the* General *advancing towards* Bouzin, Bois d'Enghien *crosses to be between them.*) What . . . NO! Yes!

(*During the following scene* Bois d'Enghien *is continually trying to get between* Bouzin *and the* General *while* Bouzin *is continually going up close to the* General.)

General. (*To* Bouzin.) So . . . You are the Poussin!
Bouzin. (*Very friendly.*) Yes indeed . . .
Bois d'Eng. (*Out of his mind.*) That's Bouzin. Yes that is . . .
General. I am delight to make with you a meet!
Bouzin. Oh so am I. Enchanted I'm sure . . .
General. Have you card?
Bouzin. Specially printed!

(Bouzin *looks for the card and passes* Bois d'Enghien *to get to the* General.)

Bois d'Eng. (*Turns away* r.) Oh my God . . .

General. My card! (*He holds it out.* Bouzin *holds his out.*)

Bouzin. (*Reading.*) General Irrigua!

General. (*Bowing.*) El Estupendo!

Bouzin. (*Bowing.*) I'm sure, General. So am I!

General. And . . . at the dawn of tomorrow . . . I have pleasure to invitation you . . . You are disposable?

Bouzin. At dawn tomorrow . . . ? Why . . . ?

General. Because I take with you to a desert part and . . . with my sword and stick you in the guts! (*Grabs him by the collar.*) Poussin!

(*The* General *shakes* Bouzin, *pulls him to his* l. *and pushes him towards the sofa.*)

Bouzin. Ooh! Why . . . why should you want to do that . . . ?

(Bois d'Enghien *crosses to* r. *of the* General *who pushes him* u. s.)

Bois d'Eng. Please . . . General . . .)

General. (*Shaking* Bouzin.) Because you are the fly in my ointments! I take you and . . . *crush* you! Under my boot! (*He twists round to the* l.) I *crush* you! Hasta la muerte!

Bouzin. Would you mind . . . ! Oh good heavens . . . !

(*The* General *pushes* Bouzin *onto the sofa.* Bois d'Enghien *crosses to the* General *to try and pull him off* Bouzin. *The* General *pushes him* u. s.)

Bois d'Eng. Now then . . . Steady on, General!

(Bois d'Enghien *crosses to doors* u. s. l. *and out into the hallway, looking for* Firmin.)

General. Leave me alone, Bodyguard. (*To* Bouzin *as*

he shakes him.) And another thing. I don't find you pretty at all. Hear me, Poussin? You are not pretty!

BOUZIN. Stop it! What a very rude fellow! Help! Help! HELP!

BOIS D'ENG. (*In the hallway.*) Help! Help!

(LUCETTE *enters* R. *and crosses to below table. The* GEN- ERAL *and* BOIS D'ENGHIEN *cross to* R. C.—*the* GEN- ERAL U. S. *of* BOIS D'ENGHIEN.)

LUCETTE. What is it? Whatever's going on?

BOUZIN. (*Regaining his balance as the* GENERAL *lets him go.*) It's this . . . gentleman!

(LUCETTE *crosses to* L. *to* BOUZIN, BOIS D'ENGHIEN *and the* GENERAL *cross* R.)

LUCETTE. Bouzin! You back again! (BOUZIN *rises and crosses below sofa to behind it.*) Please leave at once!

BOUZIN. But I've brought back my song . . .

(LUCETTE *crosses* U. S. *to* C.)

LUCETTE. Your song? Shall I tell you what I think about your song? I think it's *stupid!*

(BOUZIN *crosses* U. S. *to* LUCETTE *a little.*)

BOUZIN. Stupid?

GENERAL. (*With conviction, but without knowing what he's talking about.*) Hear that, Poussin? Your song is stupid! She told you!

LUCETTE. (*Pointing to the door.*) Please leave at once!

BOUZIN. Me?

BOIS D'ENG. She told you to leave at once. So leave at once!

GENERAL. Do you hear, Poussin? Get out!

LUCETTE. Get out!

BOIS D'ENG. Get out!

BOUZIN. (*Deeply hurt.*) It's a madhouse!

(BOUZIN *exits* U. S. L. *and everyone follows him off and returns immediately.* BOIS D'ENGHIEN *enters and crosses to above* U. R. *of table. The* GENERAL *crosses to* U. R. C. LUCETTE *slams the door and crosses* D. R. *to below table.*)

LUCETTE. (*To* BOIS D'ENGHIEN.) You just don't make fun of people like he did. It's in extremely poor taste . . .

(*The* GENERAL *crosses to* L. *of* LUCETTE *and kneels before her.*)

GENERAL. God bless you! You have removed from me the flies from my ointments.

(BOUZIN *enters* U. S. L. *and goes to the chair* R. *of sofa for his umbrella.*)

BOIS D'ENG. (*Seeing* BOUZIN.) He's back!
LUCETTE and GENERAL. Oh!
BOUZIN. (*His voice strangled with fear.*) I forgot my umbrella! (BOUZIN *rushes through the doors* U. S. L. EVERYONE *follows him.*)
EVERYONE. Get out, Bouzin! Go on! Leave at once! Clear out!

CURTAIN

ACT TWO

SCENE: BARONESS DUVERGER'S *bedroom. A large, square, rich and elegant room. Backstage* C. *are hinged quadrupled doors leading to drawing rooms.* U. S. L. *an ordinary door.* D. R. *another ordinary door.* L. *a bed canopy and curtains. (The bed has been removed for the occasion.) In place of the bed is an armchair. Against the Upstage wall,* L. *of the door, a large empty period wardrobe. To* R. *of backstage door, almost completely hidden by a six-fold screen (the Upstage leaf of which should be fixed at right angles to the back wall) a heavily laden dressing table. Below the screen a square table with a chair above it. Chairs against the wall on either side of the door* R. C. S. L. *a chaise longue, almost at right angles to the back wall and its head Upstage. (The Upstage end should be slightly raised.) Level with the* D. S. *end, a small round table on which there is an electric bell push. To* L. *of the bed canopy, a wing chair. Through the back of the bed curtains is a tulip shaped electric light fitting, normally used when one is reading in bed. A lit chandelier hangs Centre Stage. Against the back wall of the drawing room, seen through the folding doors is a mantelpiece. In this act, everyone is in evening dress.*

VIVIANNE *is discovered* D. L. *of the chaise longue, the* FRAULEIN *kneeling slightly* U. S. L. *of her.*

VIVIANNE. (*To* FRAULEIN FITZENSPIEGEL *who is pinning* VIVIANNE'S *dress.*) Wird es bald fertig sein, Fraulein?

FRAULEIN. Eine Stecknadel bitte . . .

59

VIVIANNE. Noch ein andere!

FRAULEIN. Ich komme in einen Minute. (VIVIANNE *giving her a pin.*) Ach komm! (*They laugh.*)

(*The* BARONESS *enters* U. S. C. *and crosses* C.)

B. DUVERGER. Are you ready, Vivianne dear?

VIVIANNE. When Fraulein's finished. Really she's stuck so many pins in me! I'm just like an old wall covered with broken bottles . . . Is she afraid someone's going to climb on top of me?

B. DUVERGER. A somewhat unfortunate metaphor. (*The* BARONESS *crosses* L.)

FRAULEIN. (*Rising.*) Das ist ende!

(VIVIANNE *turns to the* BARONESS.)

VIVIANNE. Oh Mama . . . Do tell Fraulein Fitzen-spiegel it's not nice of her to miss my party.

(*The* BARONESS *crosses* C. *towards the* FRAULEIN.)

B. DUVERGER. (*To the* FRAULEIN.) Of course you must stay for the party.

(*The* FRAULEIN *turns to the* BARONESS *and in to her slightly.*)

FRAULEIN. Bitte?

B. DUVERGER. (*Trying to make her understand.*) I said "Of course you must stay for the party." (*Looking at the* FRAULEIN *who hasn't understood a word.*) You must stay! For the party! Champagne! Little pink cakes! Dance! Dance? One, two, three, hop . . . (*She tries a few dance steps and the* FRAULEIN *looks at her and laughs.*) She hasn't understood a single word! "Stay for the party." It's hardly an abstruse philosophical thought . . . (*The* BARONESS *crosses* L.)

FRAULEIN. (*Smiling all the time.*) Wass soll das bedeuten?

VIVIANNE. Konnen sie wirtlich nicht bleiben?

FRAULEIN. Ach nein! (FRAULEIN *crosses* C. *to the* BARONESS. *The* BARONESS *turns to the* FRAULEIN *and in to her slightly. Speaking very fast.*) Sie sind sehr fundlich. Aber ich muss nach hauser gehen. Meine Mutter ist krank. Sonst hatte ich es mir sehr gefallt den Der Lobten kennen zu lennen.

B. DUVERGER. (*Who's listened to this avalanche of words as if she's interested.*) Ja! Ja! (*To* VIVIANNE.) What on earth's the woman talking about? I'm surprised she can understand herself.

VIVIANNE. Her Mother's ill and she wants to go home and look after her.

B. DUVERGER. Certainly. But tell her . . . I want her to come early and take you to your singing lesson tomorrow. I'll be busy and . . . Oh tell her . . .

(*The* BARONESS *tries to make the* FRAULEIN *understand by singing to her, and then turns away in disgust.*)

VIVIANNE. (*To the* FRAULEIN.) Konnen sie früh kommen und mich zu meine gestangstuden morgen.

FRAULEIN. (*To the* BARONESS.) Ja . . . Ja . . . (*The* FRAULEIN *picks up her gloves and bag from the chaise longue.*) Aufwiedersehen Mamselle . . .

VIVIANNE. (*Sits at the foot of the chaise longue.*) Aufwiedersehen.

(*The* FRAULEIN *crosses to* U. S. C. *and exits.*)

FRAULEIN. Aufwiedersehen Madame . . . (*The* BARONESS *follows her* U. S. *a little.*)

B. DUVERGER. Aufwiedersehen. Aufwiedersehen. You see, I'm beginning to speak the language. (VIVIANNE *rises and crosses* R. *and back. She takes a mirror from the table* R. *and sits on* D. S. *end of the chaise longue. The*

BARONESS *crosses to the chaise longue and sits* U. S. *of* VIVIANNE.) So, darling. The great day's come!

VIVIANNE. (*Indifferent.*) I suppose so . . .

B. DUVERGER. (*Her arms round* VIVIANNE.) Aren't you happy at the idea of being M'sieur Bois d'Enghien's lovely young wife?

(VIVIANNE *puts the mirror back.*)

VIVIANNE. I suppose he'll do.

B. DUVERGER. (*Astonished.*) What do you mean—he'll do?

VIVIANNE. I'm only marrying him to make ? husband of him.

B. DUVERGER. Good heavens! Why does anyone get married?

(VIVIANNE *rises and crosses* L.)

VIVIANNE. I suppose it's something you have to go through—like measles. You leave your Nurse and get a Fraulein, then you leave your Fraulein and get a husband . . .

(*The* BARONESS *rises.*)

B. DUVERGER. . . . Oh.

VIVIANNE. He's just another Fraulein to me.

(*The* BARONESS *crosses to the* R. *of* VIVIANNE.)

B. DUVERGER. Really! M'sieur Bois d'Enghien's a highly respectable, well brought up . . .

VIVIANNE. That's the trouble!

B. DUVERGER. What's the trouble?

VIVIANNE. I'd much rather he'd been exposed to the public.

B. DUVERGER. You mean like an actor?

VIVIANNE. I mean like a lover.

B. DUVERGER. Really, Vivianne!

VIVIANNE. Someone who's jumped in and out of a few beds, Mama!

B. DUVERGER. A bed leaper!

VIVIANNE. Imagine how proud you'd feel married to a man like that—like wearing the Croix de Guerre, it's distinguished in itself and it makes everyone else sick with jealousy.

B. DUVERGER. I mean—but why . . . ?

VIVIANNE. Because when a lot of other people want anything, it goes up in value. It's the Law of Supply and Demand.

(*The* BARONESS *turns away.*)

B. DUVERGER. (*Sarcastic.*) Romantic notions!

(VIVIANNE *crosses to the* BARONESS *and puts her arms round her.*)

VIVIANNE. I'm afraid you're a bit young to understand!

B. DUVERGER. But you'll be happy with Fernand, won't you, darling?

(VIVIANNE *crosses below the* BARONESS *to* D. S. L. *of the chaise longue.*)

VIVIANNE. If I'm not, divorce is almost a pleasure nowadays.

(*The* BARONESS *crosses* D. S. *a pace or two.*)

B. DUVERGER. Lovely state of mind to embark on marriage!

(EMILE *enters* U. S. C. *and stands by the door.*)

EMILE. M'sieur Bois d'Enghien. (EMILE *exits.*)

B. DUVERGER. Oh, show him in . . .

(BOIS D'ENGHIEN *enters* U. S. C., *gay and eager with a bouquet.*)

BOIS D'ENG. Hullo Mother-in-law.
B. DUVERGER. Hullo Son-in-law.

(BOIS D'ENGHIEN *crosses* R. *to* VIVIANNE, *kisses her hand and gives her the bouquet.*)

VIVIANNE. (*Smiling as she takes the flowers.*) Not more flowers . . . !
BOIS D'ENG. Never enough for you, my flower. (*Takes a pace* D. S. *Aside.*) I did a deal with the Florist—buy now . . . pay after the wedding . . .

(VIVIANNE *puts the bouquet on the side table. The* BARONESS *crosses to* L. *of* BOIS D'ENGHIEN.)

B. DUVERGER. Aren't you going to kiss her? It's allowed today.

(BOIS D'ENGHIEN *crosses to* VIVIANNE *and embraces her.*)

BOIS D'ENG. Of course . . . today . . . and for ever afterwards. (*He pricks himself on one of the pins in her dress.*) Oh!
VIVIANNE. Look out. I'm armed.
BOIS D'ENG. (*Sucking his finger.*) You might've warned me!

(*The* BARONESS *in close to* L. *of* BOIS D'ENGHIEN, *her face almost against his.*)

B. DUVERGER. No pins on Mother-in-law!
BOIS D'ENG. What . . . ? Oh yes, of course. (*He kisses her.*)
B. DUVERGER. No need to handle *me* with care.
BOIS D'ENG. (*Weakly.*) Splendid!

(*The* BARONESS *crosses* U. S. *to* U. S. C. L. *then back* D. C.)

B. DUVERGER. Now. Good news! Son-in-law! The Church is unfortunately fully booked for the date we mentioned so I've fixed your marriage two days earlier!

(BOIS D'ENGHIEN *crosses to* R. *of the* BARONESS.)

BOIS D'ENG. Oh good! . . . My Florist was only just saying to me . . . "Your engagement seems to be lasting for ever!" (*To* VIVIANNE.) Isn't that marvellous!

B. DUVERGER. (*At* BOIS D'ENGHIEN'S *back*.) You must make her happy . . .

BOIS D'ENG. (*Turning round*.) Make who happy . . . ?

B. DUVERGER. Vivianne of course . . . Who else?

BOIS D'ENG. No one else . . . No one else at all.

(VIVIANNE *puts the flowers on table and crosses* R. *The* BARONESS *close to* L. *of* BOIS D'ENGHIEN.)

B. DUVERGER. I mean—you may have sown a few wild oats . . . in the past, but now I'm sure you'll . . .

BOIS D'ENG. Never. Not one little oat! Not anywhere.

(VIVIANNE *turns to* BOIS D'ENGHIEN.)

B. DUVERGER. (*Under her breath to* BOIS D'ENGHIEN.) What . . . never?

BOIS D'ENGHIEN. It never ceases to amaze me! The way some chaps of my age are forever chasing girls. I always say to them "Whatever can you chaps do with those girls once you've caught them"?

VIVIANNE. (*Aside*.) Doesn't he know? (*She takes two steps* R.)

BOIS D'ENG. (*Crossing* D. S. *a pace*.) Speaking for myself . . . I've only loved one woman in all my life . . .

(VIVIANNE *moves in a little, looking hopeful*.)

VIVIANNE. Ah?

BOIS D'ENG. My Mother!

B. DUVERGER. Ah!

VIVIANNE. (*Crossing* R. *a little, aside.*) How disgusting!

BOIS D'ENG. In fact, there's practically nothing to choose between me and Joan of Arc.

VIVIANNE. You hear voices?

BOIS D'ENG. No, but I shall go to my wedding as virginal as she was when she went to the stake.

VIVIANNE. He's even worse than I thought.

BOIS D'ENG. Personally, I think a young man who jumps the gun should be put in a donkey's head. Like . . . who's that character in the play? Bottom . . . ?

B. DUVERGER. Fernand. Your language!

(BOIS D'ENGHIEN *crosses below the* BARONESS *to* D. L.)

BOIS D'ENG. Well, his name's Bottom, isn't it? Do you expect me to call him Arthur?

B. DUVERGER. Fernand! You're a pearl beyond price!

(*The* BARONESS *moves to* L. *of* VIVIANNE.)

BOIS D'ENG. (*Aside.*) Did I lay it on a bit thick? Anyway—I showed myself in a good light . . . (BOIS D'ENGHIEN *crosses* L.)

(EMILE *enters* U. S. C. *and announces.*)

EMILE. Madame. A gentleman has arrived.

B. DUVERGER. (*Crossing* U. S. *to* EMILE.) Already?

EMILE. M'sieur de Fontanet!

BOIS D'ENG. (*Aside.*) Oh my God . . . Not the fellow I met this morning?

B. DUVERGER. You know him, Fernand?

BOIS D'ENG. No. Not at all.

B. DUVERGER. I thought not. (*She crosses to the door and speaks to* EMILE.) Ask him to come in here . . .

(*Exit* EMILE.)

BOIS D'ENG. What . . . in here?

B. DUVERGER. Why not? I don't stand on ceremony with old Fontanet . . .

BOIS D'ENG. (*Aside.*) Let's hope he doesn't drop too many bricks.

EMILE. (*Enters to show in* DE FONTANET.) If M'sieur would step this way . . . ?

(EMILE *exits and* DE FONTANET *enters* U. S. *from the* L. *and crosses to the* BARONESS *and kisses her hand.*)

DE FONTANET. My dear Baroness . . .

(BOIS D'ENGHIEN *crosses* U. S. *to* DE FONTANET *and pulls him* D. L.—BOIS D'ENGHIEN *on his* R.)

BOIS D'ENG. Surprise! Surprise! How are you!

(*The* BARONESS *crosses* D. S. *level with* U. S. *end of the chaise longue.*)

DE FONTANET. (*Surprised at this greeting.*) *You're* here?

BOIS D'ENG. Of course!

B. DUVERGER. What exactly . . . ?

BOIS D'ENG. (*Under his breath to* DE FONTANET.) Mind what you say now, old fellow. (*Aloud.*) It's good old Fontanet!

B. DUVERGER. You know him after all?

BOIS D'ENG. Good heavens yes! Of course I know him!

B. DUVERGER. But you just said . . .

BOIS D'ENG. When I hadn't seen him—now I've seen him. With my own eyes. There's no mistaking him! Fontanet! My dear old friend. (*He shakes his hand.*) It's been so long . . .

DE FONTANET. But we've just had lunch together . . .

(Bois d'Enghien *takes a pace to the* Baroness.)

Bois d'Eng. Just a little . . . I wasn't very hungry.
B. Duverger. Really? Where did you two go for lunch?
De Fontanet. To Lucette's . . .

(Bois d'Enghien *crosses to* De Fontanet.)

Bois d'Eng. (*Aside.*) Quiet, you old nit wit . . .
Vivianne. Lucette who?

(Bois d'Enghien *crosses to the* l. *of the* Baroness.)

Bois d'Eng. The Cafe Lucette! It's a new restaurant that's just opened. Excellent shellfish!
De Fontanet. (*Aside.*) What on earth's he talking about?
Bois d'Eng. (*Trying to laugh, to the* Baroness *and* Vivianne.) You mean you've never been there?

(Vivianne *moves in a little.*)

B. Duverger and Vivianne. Never.

(Bois d'Enghien *crosses closer to* De Fontanet's r.)

Bois d'Eng. (*Laughing loudly to hide his anxiety.*) Can you imagine it, Fontanet? They've never been to the Cafe Lucette. Isn't it amazing?
De Fontanet. Amazing! . . . Neither have I.
Bois d'Eng. (*Winces.*) Oh . . . (*Trying to laugh it off, crosses to* l. *of the* Baroness.) Neither has he! (*Pointing at him.*) Dear old Fontanet! He's so vague . . . He goes to a restaurant, and doesn't even know what it's called! (Bois d'Enghien *pushes* De Fontanet l. *to* d. l.) Good, old, sweet natured Fontanet who doesn't even know the Cafe Lucette. (*Under his breath.*) Will you shut up, you old idiot! (*He pushes* De Fontanet *into the chair.*)

(*The* BARONESS *and* VIVIANNE *cross* C.)

B. DUVERGER. (*Laughing.*) Where did you find the Cafe Lucette?

BOIS D'ENG. (*Astonished.*) I didn't find it.

B. DUVERGER. What?

BOIS D'ENG. Oh! Where did I find it? (*To* DE FONTANET.) My *mother-in-law* is asking where I found it?

B. DUVERGER. All right. Where did you find it?

BOIS D'ENG. I heard you the first time. (*Aside.*) Why did I get involved with this ridiculous restaurant?

DE FONTANET. What restaurant?

VIVIANNE. Well?

(BOIS D'ENGHIEN *crosses* C. *to* L. *of the* BARONESS.)

BOIS D'ENG. (*Desperate.*) Well! It's rather a long way to go.

B. DUVERGER. Doesn't matter . . .

BOIS D'ENG. Well . . . All right . . . Imagine you're in the Place de l'Opera. You know do you . . . the Place de l'Opera?

B. DUVERGER. Just about!

(DE FONTANET *rises and crosses* R. *to* L. *of* BOIS D'ENGHIEN *so that all four are standing in a line—* VIVIANNE, *the* BARONESS, BOIS D'ENGHIEN *and* DE FONTANET.)

BOIS D'ENG. If you're standing like *that!* On the island in the middle of the road. You face the Opera with the Avenue behind you. (EVERYONE *looks* R. *and behind.*) Follow me? Right. About turn! (EVERYONE *turns round with their backs to the audience. Calmly.*) And then you have the Opera behind and you face the Avenue . . .

(*The* BARONESS *faces front first, followed by everyone else.*)

B. DUVERGER. I hate to interrupt, but why not start off like that?

BOIS D'ENG. Ah! . . . You might think so! But you'd never find it that way.

B. DUVERGER. I was only trying to be helpful. As a matter of fact I don't care where it is.

BOIS D'ENG. Then I needn't go on?

B. DUVERGER. I shouldn't've thought so.

(VIVIANNE *crosses* R. *to below the chaise longue.* BOIS D'ENGHIEN *moves slightly forward.*)

BOIS D'ENG. (*Aside.*) Thank God for that. (*He crosses* U. S. *to table* L. C. DE FONTANET *takes a few paces* D. L.)

DE FONTANET. (*Aside.*) Has he gone out of his mind?

B. DUVERGER. (*To* DE FONTANET.) I see there's no need to introduce you to my daughter's fiance?

DE FONTANET. *That's* your daughter's fiance?

B. DUVERGER. Of course. (*She crosses to* L. *of* VIVIANNE.) M'sieur Bois d'Enghien.

DE FONTANET. But he's . . . But he's . . . So it's you, is it, old man? You dark horse! (BOIS D'ENGHIEN *crosses* D. L. *to* R. *of* DE FONTANET.) I told you the fiance had a name like yours . . .

BOIS D'ENG. (*Aside.*) Why can't you shut up?

(*At the end of his tether, he stamps on* DE FONTANET'S *foot.* DE FONTANET *crosses* R. *hopping on his left foot,* VIVIANNE *and* BARONESS *back* R. DE FONTANET *sits* C. *of the chaise longue.*)

DE FONTANET. (*Screaming in pain.*) Oh. Ouch! Oh. Help . . . Oh . . .

EVERYONE. What's the matter?

(BOIS D'ENGHIEN *crosses* C.)

BOIS D'ENG. (*Shouting loudest.*) Come on! Tell us!

What's the matter? For God's sake, man—are you in pain? Come on. Speak up!

DE FONTANET. (*Who has limped to the sofa.*) My foot . . . My foot . . .

BOIS D'ENG. (*Aside.*) That's one way to change the subject!

DE FONTANET. (*Furious.*) You did it. With your great clod hopper!

BOIS D'ENG. I don't know what you're talking about.

DE FONTANET. On my best corn . . . (*They all lean down and look at* DE FONTANET's *foot.*)

BOIS D'ENG. You've got a corn? He has corns! How extremely unattractive!

DE FONTANET. I don't care what they look like provided you don't dance about on them . . .

VIVIANNE. (*On the other side of the chaise longue.*) Any better now, M'sieur de Fontanet?

DE FONTANET. (*Rising with difficulty.*) A little better, thank you, Mademoiselle . . . (DE FONTANET *crosses* L., *limping.* BOIS D'ENGHIEN *crosses* L.)

BOIS D'ENG. Good. Good. None of this fuss will stop us signing the marriage settlement. When the lawyer arrives. M'sieur Lantery hasn't come yet?

DE FONTANET. (*Rubbing his foot which he still can't stand on properly.*) M'sieur Lantery. Is he really your lawyer?

(*The* BARONESS *crosses to* L. *of the chaise longue.*)

B. DUVERGER. An excellent man.

BOIS D'ENG. Isn't he any good?

DE FONTANET. Oh yes. First rate. He only has one drawback, poor fellow. Terrible breath . . .

EVERYONE. (*Trying not to laugh.*) Ah . . .

DE FONTANET. Haven't you noticed? (*Breathes in* BOIS D'ENGHIEN's *face.*) Ffut! It's perfectly ghastly.

(DE FONTANET *sits on chair* D. L. BOIS D'ENGHIEN *takes a pace* D. S.)

BOIS D'ENG. (*Aside.*) How can he tell?

(EMILE *enters with a card on a salver* U. S. C.)

EMILE. There's a lady here with two—other persons. She says Madame's expecting her. Her card!

(*The* BARONESS *crosses* U. C. *to* EMILE.)

B. DUVERGER. Yes of course. I'm coming.

(*Exit* EMILE.)

BOIS D'ENG. Who is it?
B. DUVERGER. A little surprise for my guests.
DE FONTANET. Really?

(BOIS D'ENGHIEN *crosses* U. S. L.)

BOIS D'ENG. Surely you can tell me?
B. DUVERGER. Of course not. It's a surprise. You'll enjoy it, you'll see. Vivianne, come along, dear.
VIVIANNE. Yes, Mama.

(VIVIANNE *and* BARONESS *go out* U. S. C. BOIS D'ENGHIEN *accompanies them* U. S. *and then returns.*)

BOIS D'ENG. (*To* DE FONTANET.) Idiot! Every time you opened your stupid mouth, you put your foot in it.
DE FONTANET. But why should I think you were the fiance? You're Lucette Gautier's lover.

(BOIS D'ENGHIEN *moves* U. S. *to* C.)

BOIS D'ENG. Lucette! That was all over two weeks ago.

(DE FONTANET *rises and crosses* U. S. R. *a little.*)

DE FONTANET. But I saw you there this morning . . .

BOIS D'ENG. What does that prove . . . ? This morning—I'd just dropped in to have a hot toddy . . .

DE FONTANET. Oh . . .

BOIS D'ENG. (*Crossing to* DE FONTANET *who stands on one foot.*) Whatever you do . . . not a word to Lucette about this marriage. She's going to find out quite soon enough.

(*The SOUND of voices in the passage.*)

DE FONTANET. No . . . Of course not . . . (*He crosses slowly to the doors* U. S. C.) Look out . . . your Mother-in-law's coming back.

BOIS D'ENG. (*Calmly.*) With her little surprise. No doubt.

(DE FONTANET *continues to move up and through the doors, looking off* L.)

DE FONTANET. Do you think so? I'll go and see? (*He arrives in the passage and speaks to someone.*) Good heavens it's her! (*Offstage.*) Good heavens, it's you!

(BOIS D'ENGHIEN, *smitten with curiosity, crosses* U. S. *to doors and looks Offstage* L.)

BOIS D'ENG. What does he mean "You" "Her." (*He sees* LUCETTE.) Lucette Gautier! (*He dashes to door* R. *and finds it locked.*) It's locked! (*He crosses to slightly* D. S. *of centre doors.*) Lucette here! (*Driven mad, not knowing where to go, he crosses to the cupboard* U. S. R.) Ah. Thank God!

(BOIS D'ENGHIEN *gets into the cupboard and closes the doors.* DE FONTANET *backs* R. *into the doorway.*)

DE FONTANET. A surprise! What a surprise . . .

(*The* BARONESS *appears in the doorway.*)

B. DUVERGER. Isn't it? So, Mademoiselle. If you'd care to come in here . . .

DE FONTANET. (*Aside.*) Oh my God . . . The poor fellow. (*He stands in the doorway with his back to the audience, barring everyone's way. Aloud.*) No! Not in here . . .

EVERYONE. Why ever not?

DE FONTANET. Because . . . Because. (*He looks round the room and sees no* BOIS D'ENGHIEN.) Vanished! (*Aloud.*) In here then. (*He crosses* R. *to above the chaise longue.*) Come in here if you want to . . .

EVERYONE. Of course we do.

DE FONTANET. (*Aside.*) Vanished! Very wise.

(*The* BARONESS *crosses* L. C. *to above* L. *table.*)

B. DUVERGER. (*To* LUCETTE.) I hope this room'll do.

(LUCETTE *crosses* C. *and* DE CHENNEVIETTE *crosses to* U. S. *between the* BARONESS *and* LUCETTE.)

LUCETTE. It might just suit.

(MARCELINE *crosses* D. R. *of* L. *table.* VIVIANNE *crosses* U. S. *and* R. *of* MARCELINE.)

MARCELINE. You should see her pokey little dressing room at the Moulin Rouge. Powder your nose and you'll find you're dusting the ceiling . . .

B. DUVERGER. (*To* MARCELINE *who's brought in a big cardboard box.*) You can put it there, my girl.

(MARCELINE *crosses to* D. S. *end of table* L. *and puts the box on it.*)

LUCETTE. (*Introducing* DE CHENNEVIETTE *who's carrying her make-up case.*) Can I introduce M'sieur de Chenneviette . . . ? (DE CHENNEVIETTE *takes one pace* D. S.)

I brought him along. He's my oldest friend. Really he's just like a father . . . I mean . . . He's my charge d'affaires when I have engagements like this.

B. DUVERGER. How do you do?

(DE CHENNEVIETTE *puts the case on* U. S. *side of the* L. *table.*)

MARCELINE. No fear of her introducing me . . .

B. DUVERGER. I hope you'll find all you want. This is in fact my bedroom, but I've converted it . . . I tried to convert it into a dressing room fit for a great star. (*The* BARONESS *crosses* U. S. *to screen* U. L. *followed by* LUCETTE *who then crosses* R. C., *followed by* DE CHENNEVIETTE.) Washing things are behind the screen . . . (*The* BARONESS *crosses* R. *to the cupboard by* DE CHENNEVIETTE.) You can put all your costumes in this cupboard . . . (LUCETTE *crosses* U. S. *a little.*) It's quite empty.

LUCETTE. Perfect!

(*The* BARONESS *crosses to table* R. *of chaise longue, followed by* DE CHENNEVIETTE.)

B. DUVERGER. There's an electric bell on the table. Just ring if you want anything. (*She crosses to door* R.) And through here . . . Oh dear . . . Why's it locked? (*She takes two steps forward and speaks to* VIVIANNE *who's near the cupboard chatting to* DE FONTANET.) Could you go round, darling? The key's on the other side.

VIVIANNE. Yes, Mama. (*She exits* U. S. C. *and goes off* R. *The* BARONESS *crosses to above the chaise longue.*)

B. DUVERGER. It opens into the kitchen corridor . . . It'd be quicker if your personal maid goes through to the kitchen herself.

MARCELINE. (*Crosses.*) What personal maid's that?

B. DUVERGER. Aren't you the maid . . . ?

(MARCELINE *crosses* L. C. *level with* LUCETTE.)

MARCELINE. Certainly not. I'm Madame Gautier's personal sister.

B. DUVERGER. I'm so sorry . . .

MARCELINE. Say no more. (*Aside.*) I'll give you personal maid! (*She goes L. to table L.*)

(VIVIANNE *enters by the door* L.)

VIVIANNE. I've got it open . . . (*She crosses to* D. S. R. *of* DE FONTANET.)

B. DUVERGER. (*To* LUCETTE.) Now if you'd like to come into the drawing room . . . You can see where we've put your platform and the piano . . .

(LUCETTE *crosses* D. R. *to the chair under the canopy.*)

LUCETTE. No, Madame. That's my manager's business! (*To* DE CHENNEVIETTE.) Chenneviette!

DE CHENNEV. Yes, of course. (*To the* BARONESS.) If you'd like to show me . . . ?

B. DUVERGER. (*Beckoning to* DE FONTANET.) Coming, Fontanet?

(DE FONTANET *exits* U. S. *going* R. *followed by* DE CHENNEVIETTE.)

DE FONTANET. I'm at your disposal, Baroness . . .

LUCETTE. My sister'll help me unpack.

B. DUVERGER. Come along then, Vivianne. (VIVIANNE *crosses to doors* C.) Where's that fiance of yours got to?

VIVIANNE. (*Gloomily.*) Probably at prayer . . .

(*Exit* VIVIANNE *and* BARONESS U. S. C. *and to the* R. MARCELINE *takes a dress out of the box.*)

MARCELINE. Charming! Being taken for the maid . . .

LUCETTE. You haven't got the figure to play the sister . . .

MARCELINE. I think you like to see me humiliated . . .

(LUCETTE *crosses* L. *to* D. L. C.)

LUCETTE. Stop grumbling, darling—and hang up my costume. It's getting crumpled . . .

MARCELINE. (*Unpacking.*) I'm going to surprise you one day.

LUCETTE. My God, don't tell me . . .

(MARCELINE *crosses to* L. *of* LUCETTE *to* C. *of the Stage.*)

MARCELINE. I'm going to have a lover!

LUCETTE. Yes, darling . . .

MARCELINE. You've got no idea what I'm really like . . .

LUCETTE. (*Laughing.*) A lover—you? (*Change of voice.*) Careful how you hold that dress, darling . . . (*She crosses* L. *to table* L.) It's a good thing you're not a maid. (MARCELINE *crosses to cupboard* U. R., *tries to open it, puts the costume on the end of the chaise longue and tries again.*) You wouldn't keep a job long.

MARCELINE. Not with you, anyway! What's the matter with this thing? I can't open it.

LUCETTE. Try turning the key . . .

MARCELINE. I tried that! It doesn't work.

(LUCETTE *crosses below table to cupboard, pushing* MARCELINE L.)

LUCETTE. Honestly, after all that money I pay out for you to go to evening classes, and you can't open a simple cupboard. Here . . . Move yourself . . . (*She hustles* MARCELINE *out of the way—and takes her place, trying to open the cupboard.*) You're right! It's stiff! (*Rattles it.*) Open . . . you idiotic bit of furniture!

MARCELINE. I didn't lose my temper with it. (*The

doors open fractionally and then BOIS D'ENGHIEN *pulls them shut.*)

LUCETTE. (*Trying to pull it open.*) It's almost as if . . . a mysterious hidden force were pulling in the opposite direction. (*To* MARCELINE.) Let's pull together. One . . . two . . . three . . .

(MARCELINE *holds* LUCETTE's *waist and they pull together. The doors open.*)

LUCELLE and MARCELINE. There! (*The door gives—* BOIS D'ENGHIEN *almost falls on top of them.* LUCETTE *and* MARCELINE *scream.*) Ah! (*They run away terrified, too scared to look.*)

LUCETTE. A man!

MARCELINE. A burglar!

BOIS D'ENG. (*He's recovered his balance in the cupboard, and says calmly.*) It was you, wasn't it?

LUCETTE. Fernand!

MARCELINE. M'sieur Bois d'Enghien!

LUCETTE. (*Half angry, half scared.*) What on earth are you doing there?

BOIS D'ENG. (*Coming out of the cupboard.*) Me? Waiting for you . . .

LUCETTE. In the cupboard?

BOIS D'ENG. Naturally. (*He crosses* C.) There are moments in a particularly busy life, when one wishes to be alone. Everything going well?

LUCETTE. You shouldn't frighten us like that.

MARCELINE. My blood ran cold. (*Sits on chair* D. L.)

BOIS D'ENG. You were scared? (*Laughs.*) So my little joke came off . . .

(BOIS D'ENGHIEN *crosses to* R. *of* LUCETTE.)

LUCETTE. Funny man!

BOIS D'ENG. Wasn't it? I said to myself, Lucette will come in here, she'll open the cupboard . . . and we'll all have a good laugh. Clever, wasn't it.

LUCETTE. Was it?

MARCELINE. If you ask me, it was extremely silly!

BOIS D'ENG. Thanks very much. (*He crosses to below chaise longue.*) Just so long as the others don't come in . . .

(DE CHENNEVIETTE *enters* U. S. *from* R. *and crosses* D. S. MARCELINE *crosses to the top of the chaise longue and puts the costume in the cupboard.*)

DE CHENNEV. It's all ready in there . . .

BOIS D'ENG. (*Crossing to the* R. *of* DE CHENNEVIETTE.) Chenneviette!

DE CHENNEV. Bois d'Enghien! Where did you come from?

LUCETTE. The cupboard.

DE CHENNEV. The what!

(BOIS D'ENGHIEN *crosses* D. L. *below* DE CHENNEVIETTE *and* LUCETTE.)

BOIS D'ENG. (*Unconvincingly.*) I was in the cupboard. (*He grins.*) Playing a merry little prank . . .

DE CHENNEV. (*Aside.*) The man's a lunatic!

(MARCELINE *crosses to the chaise longue.*)

MARCELINE. (*Carrying the costume's cardboard box.*) I'll take this out of here . . .

(DE CHENNEVIETTE *crosses* U. S. R. *to level with* L. *of the chaise longue.*)

DE CHENNEV. Oh good . . .

MARCELINE. By the servant's entrance . . . (MARCELINE *exits* R.)

LUCETTE. (*To* BOIS D'ENGHIEN.) So you know the Duvergers?

BOIS D'ENG. (*Calmly.*) Oh yes, for years. I knew the Mother when she was so high!

EVERYONE. What!

BOIS D'ENG. (*Thinks again.*) I mean, the Mother knew me when I was so high . . .

LUCETTE. Funny man!

BOIS D'ENG. (*Grinning.*) Aren't I . . . a perfect scream. (*Unsmiling and moving quickly to the* R.) And now will you be so kind as not to sing in this house. Understand?

LUCETTE. (*Astonished.*) Not sing! Whyever not?

BOIS D'ENG. Whyever not? You want to know whyever not . . . ?

LUCETTE. Yes!

BOIS D'ENG. Because . . . Well because. It's an old house. Built in the eighteenth century. It's extremely draughty!

LUCETTE. Draughty? Where?

BOIS D'ENG. The wind comes howling under the front door, sweeps straight up the hall, whistles into the drawing room . . . and you'll find your platform's freezing.

(DE CHENNEVIETTE *crosses* D. R.)

LUCETTE. My platform freezing! (*She crosses* U. R. *to* DE CHENNEVIETTE, BOIS D'ENGHIEN *takes her hand and turns her round.*) I'll see the Baroness about it.

BOIS D'ENG. That'd be telling tales . . . She'll blame me and . . .

LUCETTE. I won't breathe a word about you. (BOIS D'ENGHIEN *crosses* D. L. *We see the* BARONESS *approaching* U. S.) Here she comes! I'll have it out with her.

BOIS D'ENG. (*Rushing to the* L.) Mother-in-law! I'm off . . .

LUCETTE. Where're you going?

BOIS D'ENG. (*In the doorway.*) Remember . . . you haven't seen me! (*He exits door* D. L.)

LUCETTE. Comical fellow!

DE CHENNEVIETTE. (*Who's been watching this scene*

with profound astonishment, aside.) It'll be interesting to
see how all this ends . . .

(*The* BARONESS *enters* U. S. C. *from the* R. *and crosses to*
C. *to* R. *of* LUCETTE. DE CHENNEVIETTE *crosses to*
D. S. R. *of the* BARONESS.)

B. DUVERGER. Did my son-in-law come through here?

LUCETTE. Madame. I wanted to see you. It seems that
you have draughts in your drawing room.

B. DUVERGER. In *my* drawing room!

LUCETTE. (*Polite, but firm.*) So I have heard. And it's
just not possible to sing with a howling gale blowing
down the back of your neck.

B. DUVERGER. (*Very upset. Speaking first to* LUCETTE
and then to DE CHENNEVIETTE.) I really don't know
what you're talking about! A howling gale. Really,
M'sieur, in my drawing room! Mademoiselle! Come and
see if you can find the smallest breath of air . . .

LUCETTE. All right! We'll go and see. I tell you. I don't
accept engagements north of the Arctic Circle . . .

B. DUVERGER. This way. Please. (*As they go* U. S.) A
howling gale. In my drawing room. What an extraordinary
suggestion!

(*The* BARONESS *exits* U. S. C. *followed by* LUCETTE *and*
they go off R. DE CHENNEVIETTE *crosses to door* L.)

DE CHENNEV. Oh dear, oh dear, oh dear. And she won't
find the smallest whisper of a draught . . .

(BOIS D'ENGHIEN *enters through door* R. *and crosses* L.
to R. *of* DE CHENNEVIETTE.)

BOIS D'ENG. Oof. You're alone.

DE CHENNEV. You came from there?

BOIS D'ENG. Because I went from there! (*Long ad lib*
describing "the tour" at this point.) . . . And made a
complete tour of the establishment!

DE CHENNEV. Would it be too much to ask you what the hell's going on?

BOIS D'ENG. What's going on? Total disaster! I'm about to sign my marriage settlement and celebrate my engagement and Lucette's here! That's what's going on . . .

DE CHENNEV. You don't mean it?

BOIS D'ENG. What do you mean I don't mean it . . . Of course I mean it . . .

DE CHENNEV. (*Hits his chest.*) They'll explode!

(*He's half turned his back to* BOIS D'ENGHIEN *with this movement.* BOIS D'ENGHIEN *pushes* DE CHENNE-VIETTE *half round* [*i.e.* DE CHENNEVIETTE *has his back to* BOIS D'ENGHIEN].)

BOIS D'ENG. You've got to stop it. (BOIS D'ENGHIEN *pulls him through the rest of the circular move so that* DE CHENNEVIETTE *faces him again.*) Get Lucette out of here . . .

DE CHENNEV. How?

BOIS D'ENG. By fair means or foul!

DE CHENNEV. I'll try . . . (*He half turns away again, as before.*)

BOIS D'ENG. (*Spins him round as before.*) Where is she now?

DE CHENNEV. (*Angry at being spun round.*) In the Baroness' drawing room. Trying to get to the bottom of your howling gale . . . (DE CHENNEVIETTE *crosses u. s. to l. of centre doors.*)

BOIS D'ENG. I'm afraid . . . that little trick won't stand up much longer . . . (*SOUND of voices in the passage.*) It's fallen down already.

DE CHENNEV. Here they come . . .

BOIS D'ENG. Oh . . .

(BOIS D'ENGHIEN *crosses to door* L. *and bumps into* VIVIANNE *as she enters.*)

BOIS D'ENGHIEN and VIVIANNE. Oh . . .

(*They are shoulder to shoulder.* VIVIANNE D. S. *and* BOIS D'ENGHIEN U. S.)

BOIS D'ENG. Oh my God! (*Laughs nervously.*) It's you!

VIVIANNE. I've been looking for you for the last half hour . . . (DE CHENNEVIETTE *crosses* D. S. *to* L. *of middle of chaise longue.*)

BOIS D'ENG. So have I! (*Trying to get her out.*) Let's look for us together!

VIVIANNE. (*Holding him.*) But we've found us!

BOIS D'ENG. So we have! (*Aside.*) I've lost the thread of this conversation.

DE CHENNEV. The poor boy's delirious.

(*We hear the* BARONESS' *VOICE.*)

B. DUVERGER. Wasn't I right, Mademoiselle?

LUCETTE. As a matter of fact, you were.

DE CHENNEVIETTE and BOIS D'ENG. It's them!

(VIVIANNE *takes two steps to the* R. *The* BARONESS *enters* U. S. C. *and crosses to* C. LUCETTE *enters* U. S. C. *and crosses to the* R. *of the* BARONESS. BOIS D'ENGHIEN *creeps to the door* L.)

B. DUVERGER. (*At the moment that* BOIS D'ENGHIEN *is disappearing.*) Ah! Bois d'Enghien! There you are at last!

(*The* BARONESS *crosses to* L. *below table.* BOIS D'ENG-HIEN *spins round on his toes.*)

BOIS D'ENG. Yes? There I am . . . at last.

B. DUVERGER. (*To* LUCETTE.) Mademoiselle . . .

BOIS D'ENG. (*Aside.*) Take cover, everyone . . .

B. DUVERGER. (*To* LUCETTE—*who's already smiling at* BOIS D'ENGHIEN.) May I introduce . . .

(DE CHENNEVIETTE *crosses to* U. S. *of* LUCETTE *and tries to drag her off.*)

DE CHENNEV. Don't bother. She knows him perfectly well . . .

EVERYONE. What?

(*General TUMULT.*)

DE CHENNEV. Come with me!

LUCETTE. Where to?

DE CHENNEV. To find the draught. I know where it is!

LUCETTE. (*Being pulled out by* DE CHENNEVIETTE.) What . . . Now . . . Steady on . . . Steady on . . . Leave me alone.

DE CHENNEVIETTE. Come and find the draught!

(*Exit* DE CHENNEVIETTE U. S. *dragging* LUCETTE *with him, they go.* VIVIANNE *crosses* U. S. L.)

BOIS D'ENG. (*Aside, gleefully.*) It's a reprieve!

B. DUVERGER. Why did he drag her off in that extraordinary manner?

BOIS D'ENG. Why? Why did he do that? (*He strides up between the* BARONESS *and* VIVIANNE *and takes them both by the hand and drags them back* D. S.) He did that, Madame—to stop you putting your foot right in it.

B. DUVERGER. My foot . . . in where?

VIVIANNE. What *do* you mean?

BOIS D'ENG. I have a ghastly suspicion that you were about to introduce me as "your future-son-in-law" or "your daughter's fiancé" or some such words . . .

B. DUVERGER. Of course I was!

BOIS D'ENG. Fatal! Fatal! Poor Lucette Gautier! She'd have gone stark staring mad . . . You'd've had a raving singer on your hands . . . It's just enough to mention the words "future-son-in-law" or "fiancé" to her to start her off.

B. DUVERGER. Why?

BOIS D'ENG. Why? Well because. Because . . . The gentleman who was here told me all about it! It seems there was—an unhappy love affair!

VIVIANNE. (*Interested.*) Oh do go on!

BOIS D'ENG. (*Moved.*) An extraordinarily handsome young man. She adored him! In fact they were going to get married. Unfortunately he suffered from a certain defect of character. He couldn't pay his rent so . . . (*With a sigh.*) One fine day he succumbed . . .

B. DUVERGER. Consumption . . . ?

BOIS D'ENG. A rich American widow . . .

B. DUVERGER. Oh dear . . .

BOIS D'ENG. . . . So . . . Lucette's marriage went up in smoke—and if she ever hears the words fiance or future son-in-law, I mean that gentlemen did warn me— she's lucky if she gets away with a prolonged nervous breakdown . . .

B. DUVERGER. How terrible!

VIVIANNE. What a romantic story.

BOIS D'ENG. So not a word—eh?

B. DUVERGER. Thank heavens you warned us!

(BOIS D'ENGHIEN *is moving* U. S. *to keep a look out.*)

VIVIANNE. Yes . . . Thank heavens . . .

(*NOISES Off.*)

BOIS D'ENG. It's them! Come with me!

(BOIS D'ENGHIEN *takes* VIVIANNE *with his* L. *hand, the* BARONESS *with his* R. *and pulls them to door* L.)

B. DUVERGER and VIVIANNE. Whatever for?

BOIS D'ENG. I've got something else to tell you . . . I mean show you. It's upstairs. You see? Upstairs. Yes. Come on.

(*He pushes the* BARONESS *and* VIVIANNE *out of the door*
  L. DE CHENNEVIETTE *and* LUCETTE *enter* U. S. C.
  LUCETTE *sits on the chaise longue,* DE CHEN-
  NEVIETTE *crosses to* D. R.)

LUCETTE. (*To* DE CHENNEVIETTE.) You can't go round
looking as if you were a Sanitary Inspector. You're really
being very stupid.

DE CHENNEVIETTE. (*Aside.*) It's that wretched Bois
d'Enghien. He's cast me as the bloody fool.

DE FONTANET. (*Enters* U. S. C. *and crosses* L. C.)
Promise me I'm not in the way . . . ?

LUCETTE. (*Starting to powder her face—looking at herself in the hand mirror.*) Of course not.

DE FONTANET. I'm getting so bored. Everyone goes off
and leaves me. Just as if I were contagious, or something . . .

LUCETTE. Poor old Fontanet!

DE FONTANET. It's most irritating!

(EMILE *enters and announces.*)

EMILE. General Irrigua!

DE FONTANET. Whoever's that?

LUCETTE. Oh him!

DE CHENNEV. Good God. Did someone invite that
appalling dago?

LUCETTE. Yes, darling. I did. (*To the* GENERAL *as he
appears* U. S.) There you are, General . . .

(*The* GENERAL *enters* U. S. C. *from* L. *and crosses to* L. *of*
  LUCETTE *hurriedly, with a bouquet in his hand.*)

GENERAL. I'm late. This is not forgiven me. All time is
rubbish away from you . . .

LUCETTE. As a matter of fact you're not late at all.

DE CHENNEV. Hullo General.

GENERAL. (*Nods to him.*) Buenos Dias. (*He nods to*

DE FONTANET *who nods back. He presents the bouquet
to* LUCETTE—*cornstalks with wild flowers.*) Allow me to
make the offering . . . Uno, dos, tres!

LUCETTE. (*Without taking them.*) Wild flowers . . .
charming notion!

GENERAL. That's what I am thinking. (*Shows the
bouquet.*) Simple ears of corn . . . And Marigolds!
(LUCETTE *looks at* DE FONTANET *and* DE CHEN-
NEVIETTE.) Marigolds . . . I make a comico joke. Marigolds. So if you have me you will marry gold!

LUCETTE. It's a joke!

EVERYONE. How charming!

GENERAL. (*Satisfied.*) I am astonishing witty.

DE CHENNEV. (*Flattering.*) Very Parisian. (*Aside.*)
For a Red Indian . . .

GENERAL. But the bouquet is well wrapped!

ALL. Ah!

(LUCETTE *puts down the mirror and takes the flowers
being offered to her by the* GENERAL, *then gives the
bouquet to* DE CHENNEVIETTE *who puts it on the
table* R.)

LUCETTE. (*Unwrapping the pearl necklace that sur-
rounds the flower stems.*) A pearl necklace . . . really,
General!

GENERAL. A merely bacatil! (*He crosses* L. *to* DE
FONTANET.)

DE FONTANET. (*To the* GENERAL.) May I . . . ?

(DE FONTANET *crosses* R. *to* L. *of* LUCETTE.)

EVERYONE. They're gorgeous!

DE CHENNEV. Good heavens, yes!

(LUCETTE *rises and crosses to* D. S. *end of the chaise
longue.* DE CHENNEVIETTE *puts the necklace on
her.*)

LUCETTE. You've no idea how much I love them.

DE FONTANET. They show taste. I find them in excellent taste. (*Takes a pace towards the* GENERAL.) Deeds, not words, eh?

LUCETTE. (*Introducing* DE FONTANET *without moving away from* DE CHENNEVIETTE.) General. This is M'sieur Ignace de Fontanet . . .

(DE CHENNEVIETTE *holds the mirror for* LUCETTE *to see the necklace.*)

GENERAL. (*Holding out his hand.*) Delightful . . .

DE FONTANET. I congratulate you, General. Such a magnificent gesture.

GENERAL. (*Getting a blast of* DE FONTANET'S *breath.*) Not another word—I beg you!

(*The* GENERAL *backs* D. L., DE FONTANET *still shaking his hand, follows.*)

DE FONTANET. It's marvellous to find a millionaire in love. I mean so many millionaires aren't in love and so many lovers aren't millionaires . . . it seems unfair really.

GENERAL. Si! Si! (*Takes a small box out of his waistcoat pocket.*) Have a peppermint?

DE FONTANET. Whatever for?

GENERAL. I always take a peppermint after smoking the cigaros.

DE FONTANET. (*In the* GENERAL'S *face.*) I never smoke cigaros.

GENERAL. (*Waves his hat in front of his face, apparently regretfully but really to waft away the fumes. Crosses below* DE FONTANET *to his* R.) Caramba! I insist you have a peppermint.

DE FONTANET. (*Taking one.*) Just to please you. (DE FONTANET *backs* U. S.)

GENERAL. Muchas gracias. (*Sees the* BARONESS DUVERGER *entering* R. *He goes up to her relieved, saying for* DE FONTANET.) Excuse please!

B. DUVERGER. (*As she enters* L.) I can offer no explanation for the fact that my daughter's fiance dragged us up three flights of stairs in order to point out that this house has no lightning conductor! (*She shuts the door.*)

(*The* GENERAL *takes two steps* L.)

GENERAL. Madame!

(DE CHENNEVIETTE *puts the mirror on the table, and crosses* R.)

LUCETTE. Madame. (*She takes two steps* L.) May I introduce you to my dear friend, General Irrigua?

GENERAL. El Estupendo!

LUCETTE. He was pleased to accept one of your invitation cards.

GENERAL. (*Showing his card.*) I have address it to myself in person!

B. DUVERGER. You needn't have bothered. We're just having a little family gathering . . .

GENERAL. (*As if he were extremely polite.*) Help yourself. (*The* GENERAL *slaps the* BARONESS'S *behind and crosses to* L. *of* LUCETTE.) For me, I only came here to see Mademoiselle Gautier . . .

B. DUVERGER. Oh, did you? (*Aside while the* GENERAL *is talking to* LUCETTE.) Delightful manners . . . !

(*The* BARONESS *crosses* U. S. *to* L. *of* DE FONTANET. VIVIANNE *comes in to below chair by the table* L. BOIS D'ENGHIEN *stays by the door* L.)

VIVIANNE. Come along. What's the matter with you this evening?

BOIS D'ENG. What . . . ? Oh nothing at all. (*Aside.*) Oh, good. The General.

GENERAL. (*Recognising* BOIS D'ENGHIEN.) Buenos dias, Bodyguard! What're you going to sing for us tonight?

EVERYONE. What's he going to sing?
GENERAL. He the tenor voice.
LUCETTE. Him!
EVERYONE. No!
VIVIANNE. What—you actually sing?
BOIS D'ENG. Hardly at all.

(*The* GENERAL *crosses* R. *above chaise longue to* U. S. L.
of DE CHENNEVIETTE. VIVIANNE *crosses* U. S. *to* R.
of BOIS D'ENGHIEN.)

VIVIANNE. And I never knew . . . wonderful! We'll be
able to make music together . . . in the evenings! (*She
crosses to* L. *of* BARONESS.)
BOIS D'ENG. (*Aside.*) What a lovely way to spend the
evenings.

(EMILE *and a* LACKEY *open both* U. S. C. *doors.*)

EMILE. (*Announces.*) M'sieur Lantery!

(*The* BARONESS *crosses* U. S. *to bring in* LANTERY.)

BARONESS. Our dear lawyer! Welcome, M'sieur Lan-
tery . . .
LANTERY. (*Entering and moving* D. S.) Dear Baroness.
M'sieurs . . . Mesdames . . .

(*The* BARONESS *crosses to* L. C. *with* LANTERY.)

B. DUVERGER. Can we begin right away? You've
brought the marriage settlement?
LANTERY. My articled clerk is bringing it in. (*He turns*
U. S.) Ah . . . here he is . . .

(BOUZIN *appears* U. S. *talking to* EMILE.)

B. DUVERGER. Excellent!

Bois d'Eng. (*Aside as he crosses* R. *to* Lucette.) Oh hell . . . Bouzin's arrived. (*To* Lucette.) What's Bouzin doing here?

Lucette. Bouzin. My God! If the General spots him!

(*She crosses* R. *to* D. S. *of the* General. Bois d'Enghien *crosses* D. L. *and shakes hands with* Lantery. Lucette *starts chattering to the* General, *her back to the audience—so that he has to turn round. The* Baroness *indicates* Bois d'Enghien. *She moves* U. S. *with* Lantery *towards* Bouzin.)

B. Duverger. If you'd like to come up here, my friends . . . and we'll read out the marriage settlement.

De Fontanet and Vivianne and Bois d'Eng. Yes, of course . . . Very well . . .

(Lantery *crosses* L. *to the door.* De Fontanet *and* Vivianne *cross* U. S. *to by* U. S. C. *doors.*)

B. Duverger. M'sieur de Chenneviette?

De Chennev. (*Who has been talking to the* General.) It'd be an honour. (*To the* General.) Excuse me? (De Chenneviette *crosses* U. S. *to above chaise longue.*)

General. Scramba Cheviot! (*He goes on chattering to* Lucette.)

(*The* Baroness *crosses to* U. S. *doors.*)

B. Duverger. (*To* Bouzin *in the second room.*) It's the gentleman I saw this morning . . .

Bouzin. The Baroness . . . Yes, it's me. So I'm among friends . . .

B. Duverger. Yes, of course you are . . . (*To* Lucette.) Mademoiselle, won't you come too?

Lucette. (*Startled.*) *What?* No, thank you. Madame. I've got to make my little preparations. (*She crosses* U. S.)

B. Duverger. As you wish . . .

Bois d'Eng. (*Sighs with relief.*) Oof!

B. Duverger. (*To the* General.) General?

General. Scramba Madame. I am liking to stay with Mademoiselle Gautier.

(De Chenneviette, De Fontanet, Lantery, Vivianne, *the* Baroness *cross into the corridor above* u. s. c. *doors.*)

B. Duverger. (*Aside.*) Of course you are. (*Aloud.*) Come along, Bois d'Enghien.

(*The* Baroness *exits off* r. *followed by* De Fontanet, Lantery, Vivianne *into the corridor.*)

Bois d'Eng. Coming!

(*He crosses to* u. s. c. *doors.* Lucette *begins taking her costume out of the cupboard.*)

Lucette. You're not going in there, are you?

Bois d'Eng. (*Trapped.*) Why should I?

(Lucette *crosses* d. s. *to* l. *of the chaise longue.*)

Lucette. Do marriage settlements interest you?

Bois d'Eng. Me? I find them very boring actually . . .

General. They bore me too. So we stay! Bueno!

Bois d'Eng. Bueno!

General. Good!

Bois d'Eng. Oh good heavens, no! (*He crosses* d. s. *to* d. s. c. *Aside.*) How am I going to get out of signing my own marriage settlement?

Lucette. If you like, you can go in there later.

Bois d'Eng. (*Eagerly.*) Yes!

Lucette. With me. (*She hands her bodice to the* General *who puts it on the chair* r.)

Bois d'Eng. That'd be charming.

EVERYONE. (*Calling out in the passage.*) Bois d'Enghien! Bois d'Enghien!

BOIS D'ENG. (*Crossing U. S. to door.*) I'm coming!

LUCETTE. They seem to want you . . .

(BOIS D'ENGHIEN *crosses D. S. to C.*)

BOIS D'ENG. (*Pretends to laugh.*) What on earth for? That's what I ask myself . . .

(*The* BARONESS *enters U. S. C. and crosses C.* DE CHENNEVIETTE *enters U. S. C. and crosses U. S. R. of the chaise longue, followed by* MARCELINE *who crosses to U. S. L. of him.* VIVIANNE *and* DE FONTANET *enter U. S. C. and cross U. L.—*DE FONTANET *on* VIVIANNE'S *R.* BOUZIN *enters U. S. C. and crosses U. L. to chair L. of table.*)

B. DUVERGER. Come along, Bois d'Enghien. Whatever's keeping you? (*Points to* BOUZIN *who's gone to the table L.*) This gentleman's waiting to read the marriage settlement.

(*The* GENERAL *recognises* BOUZIN *and crosses to him.* BOUZIN *knocks over a chair.*)

GENERAL. Poussin!

BOUZIN. The General's here! Help!

GENERAL. Poussin here! Poussin there! Poussin every places. You're a dead corpse, Poussin!

(*The* GENERAL *crosses round the table,* BOUZIN *backing. The latter hides behind the* BARONESS, *pushing her round twice, chased by the* GENERAL. BOUZIN *pushes* BOIS D'ENGHIEN *U. S. to L. of table, crosses to L., knocks over a chair D. L. and exits D. L. The* GENERAL *leaps over the chair and exits D. S. During the chase,* LUCETTE *and* MARCELINE *hug each other*

U. S. *of the chair covered by the canopy.* DE FON-
TANET *crosses to* U. R. *and* VIVIANNE *turns her back
to* EVERYONE.)

B. DUVERGER. What's happening. Are we at War?

LUCETTE. It's all right, Madame! De Chenneviette, for
God's sake . . . separate them!

DE CHENNEV. I'll try.

(DE CHENNEVIETTE *crosses* D. L. *to door and exits, pushing* BOIS D'ENGHIEN *to* C. MARCELINE *sits on the
chair under the canopy. Amid the tumult,* BOUZIN
enters U. S. C. *and crosses two paces* D. S. *He sees the*
BARONESS *and screams. He exits* D. L. *pursued by
the* GENERAL *and* DE CHENNEVIETTE. MARCELINE
rises and clasps LUCETTE *again,* VIVIANNE *crosses to*
BOIS D'ENGHIEN *and embraces him. The* BARONESS
crosses to the R. *of the table* L.)

B. DUVERGER. What's happening? Who's he? Why are
they chasing that gentleman? Have they started another
demonstration?

(LUCETTE *crosses* L. *to* L. *of middle of the chaise longue.*)

LUCETTE. Please, Madame. Pay no attention . . .

(*The* BARONESS *crosses two steps* R. *to* C.)

B. DUVERGER. I'd planned a simple family gathering . . . (*Then in a commanding voice.*) Now we've had
quite enough running about! Control yourselves, please.
You're all getting over-excited! We've got that marriage
settlement to read. Bois d'Enghien—take my daughter's
arm and come along.

(*The* BARONESS *crosses one step* U. S.)

LUCETTE. (*Surprised.*) Why ask him?

B. DUVERGER. (*On the spur of the moment.*) Because he's her fiance of course . . .

LUCETTE. He's . . . he's her . . . (*Screams loudly.*) Aah!

(LUCETTE *collapses on the chaise longue.* MARCELINE *crosses to* R. *of the chaise longue to catch her.*)

EVERYONE. What's the matter with her?

(BOIS D'ENGHIEN *crosses to the chaise longue and puts* LUCETTE'S *feet on the chaise longue, and kneels beside her.*)

MARCELINE. Help . . . Help . . . My poor sister . . . She's fainted!

(BOIS D'ENGHIEN *rises and crosses to* R. *of the* BARONESS.)

BOIS D'ENG. You did it! Congratulations!

B. DUVERGER. I . . .

VIVIANNE. Yes, you!

BOIS D'ENG. Don't say I didn't warn you . . . (*He crosses to kneel* L. *of* LUCETTE, DE FONTANET *crosses to* U. S. *of* MARCELINE.)

VIVIANNE. Mama! He told you not to mention the word "fiance."

(*The* GENERAL *enters* U. S. *and crosses* D. S. C. *to* R. *of the* BARONESS. DE CHENNEVIETTE *enters* U. S. *and crosses to* U. S. *of chaise longue.*)

GENERAL. I'm cutting off your life lines to escape— Poussin!

DE CHENNEV. (*Aside.*) Charming party this turned out to be!

GENERAL. (*Seeing* LUCETTE *on the sofa.*) Dios! (*He*

crosses to BOIS D'ENGHIEN *and pushes him* C. *and crosses
to* L. *of* LUCETTE.) Lucette . . . She's dying . . . my
little flower of passion . . .

BOIS D'ENG. (*Clapping his hands.*) Quick, everyone.
Vinegar! Smelling salts. Burnt feathers. Boiling water
. . . Camomile tea!

MARCELINE. I'll go. (*She exits* R. *The* BARONESS *and*
VIVIANNE *cross to behind the screen. The* GENERAL
stoops, patting LUCETTE'S *hand.*)

GENERAL. Come back with me. Mademoiselle Gautier,
darling . . . Mia amado . . . Come back to your little
Jesu-Marie Irrigua . . .

DE FONTANET. (*Breathing over her from the* R. *of the
chaise longue.*) She needs some fresh air.

(BOIS D'ENGHIEN *crosses to* U. S. *of chaise longue, having
taken salts from the* BARONESS.)

BOIS D'ENG. Well, *you'd* better get away for a start . . .

(DE CHENNEVIETTE *and* GENERAL *push* DE FONTANET
away.)

GENERAL and DE CHENNEV. Yes . . . Get away from
her . . . Get away!

BOIS D'ENG. (*To the* BARONESS *and* VIVIANNE.) We'll
go in and sign the marriage settlement.

(BOIS D'ENGHIEN, *the* BARONESS *and* VIVIANNE *cross to
the doors* U. S. *With the exception of* BOIS D'ENGHIEN
they exit off R.)

EVERYONE. Excellent! Good idea!

GENERAL. (*Commandingly.*) Alto! Stopping yourselves! Who has a key?

(BOIS D'ENGHIEN *crosses* D. R. *to the* GENERAL.)

BOIS D'ENG. (*Without thinking he hands him a key.*)
Here . . . Whatever do you want it for?

GENERAL. Gracias! (*He puts it down* LUCETTE'S *back.*)
BOIS D'ENG. She hasn't got a nose bleed . . .
GENERAL. Da nada! All the same.
BOIS D'ENG. It's the key of my private apartment . . .

(*The* BARONESS *reappears in the doorway.*)

B. DUVERGER. (*Impatient.*) Come along now. We've
got work to do . . . (*She exits and* BOIS D'ENGHIEN
crosses U. S. *and exits off* R.)
BOIS D'ENG. (*Like a man torn in half.*) Coming! Coming! (*Aside.*) I sign . . . and I shall return.
GENERAL. Si! Presto! Agua . . . Vinegar . . . Oleo
. . . Anything liquido . . .
DE FONTANET. Wait a moment! (*He crosses* U. S. L. *to
behind the screen.*)
GENERAL. Come back with me . . . Come back,
Mademoiselle Gautier, darling . . .

(DE FONTANET *crosses* R. *to above the chaise longue with
a handkerchief soaked in toilet water.*)

DE FONTANET. Here you are . . .
GENERAL. Gracias. (*Mopping* LUCETTE'S *brow.*) Come
back to me, Gautier. About turn! Quick march! Alto!
Retorgno! Presto! Uno! Duo! Tres!!!
DE FONTANET. Shall I give her the kiss of life?
DE CHENNEVIETTE and GENERAL. Certainly not!

(DE CHENNEVIETTE *pushes* DE FONTANET *against the
cupboard. The latter crosses to* D. L. C.)

DE FONTANET. You know what I personally think had
a lot to do with it? I think it was Bois d'Enghien's marriage. I could easily be wrong.
DE CHENNEV. (*Aside.*) Oh please . . . Be careful . . .
GENERAL. (*Still patting* LUCETTE'S *hands, to* DE
FONTANET.) The Tenor's making a marriage? What's
that got to do with Lucette Gautier?

DE FONTANET. Don't you know . . . he's her lover.

GENERAL. (*Leaping up and dropping the handkerchief on* LUCETTE'S *face.*) What you say?

DE CHENNEV. (*Aside.*) The old nincompoop! Oh . . . (*He takes the handkerchief off* LUCETTE'S *face and goes on tapping her hands.*)

(*The* GENERAL *crosses to the* R. *of* DE FONTANET *and pushes him* L., *shaking him by the throat.*)

GENERAL. What you say? *Bodyguard?* The lover!

DE FONTANET. Yes, of course. (*Full in the* GENERAL'S *face.*) What's the matter with you?

GENERAL. Pff! (*Gets a blast of bad breath and goes on shaking with his face averted.*) *Bodyguard* is the lover?

DE FONTANET. (*Half strangled.*) Help! Help! Bois d'Enghien! Bois d'Enghien!

(BOIS D'ENGHIEN *enters* U. S. *and crosses to the* L. *of* LUCETTE.)

BOIS D'ENG. (*Coming in gaily.*) Well now, is she any better?

(DE FONTANET *crosses* U. S. *and exits off* R. *at a run through* U. S. C. *doors.*)

DE FONTANET. Oh dear! I made a bloomer!

(*The* GENERAL *crosses to* BOIS D'ENGHIEN *and pushes him* R. *catching him by the throat.*)

GENERAL. You are the lover!

BOIS D'ENG. (*Suffocating.*) Pardon me!

GENERAL. (*Shaking him.*) I said you are the lover . . . !

BOIS D'ENG. That'll be quite enough of that . . .

DE CHENNEV. (*Trying to calm them down without leaving* LUCETTE.) Steady on, old man . . .

GENERAL. (*Throwing* BOIS D'ENGHIEN *off.*) Bodyguard. You are an appalling dago!

BOIS D'ENG. Me?

GENERAL. Yes you! And I am going to kill you! (*He goes back to* LUCETTE *and pats her hands.*)

BOIS D'ENG. (*Angry.*) Charming! Kill *me*. Whatever for?

GENERAL. (*Going back to him and shouting.*) Because you are the flies in my ointments!

BOIS D'ENG. (*Shouting louder.*) Can't you understand? I'm getting married! And you can have Lucette, for ever!

GENERAL. (*Suddenly calm.*) Verdad? That's true?

BOIS D'ENG. (*Shouting each syllable.*) Me . . . I'm getting married!

GENERAL. Bueno! You are getting married. You don't love her!

BOIS D'ENG. No!

(LUCETTE *opens her eyes, sits up slightly then lies down again closing them.*)

GENERAL. Pass, friend amigo! (*The* GENERAL *embraces* BOIS D'ENGHIEN.)

DE CHENNEV. You might like to know—she's opening her eyes.

(*The* GENERAL *crosses a pace to* LUCETTE. BOIS D'ENGHIEN *crosses to the* GENERAL *and pushes him* U. S. *to the door.* DE CHENNEVIETTE *follows the* GENERAL *off—a* LACKEY *closing the doors.*)

BOIS D'ENG. Leave me alone with her. I'd like to have a last shot . . . at saying "goodbye."

GENERAL. Bueno. I leave . . . (*To* LUCETTE *as he goes.*) Come back to him. Gautier! Returno! Presto uno! Dos! Tres! Alto. Back to him.

(*They go* U. S. C. *and* BOIS D'ENGHIEN *closes the doors on them as they leave.* LUCETTE *sits up.*)

LUCETTE. (*Coming to.*) Where am I?

(BOIS D'ENGHIEN *crosses to* LUCETTE *and kneels.*)

BOIS D'ENG. Lucette . . .

LUCETTE. (*In a pitiful voice, her hands on his shoulders.*) It's you . . . It's you, my darling!

BOIS D'ENG. Lucette. Forgive me. I behaved like a complete . . .

(LUCETTE'S *expression changes as she remembers what happened.*)

LUCETTE. Don't say it! Not another word! It's too horrible! (*She rises and moves* L. BOIS D'ENGHIEN *follows her on his knees.*)

BOIS D'ENG. Lulu. (*He rises and moves closer to* LUCETTE.) My little Lulu!

LUCETTE. (*Her voice strangled with emotion.*) So it's true! *Your* engagement party! *Your* marriage settlement! *Your* . . . little sparrow of a fiancee!

BOIS D'ENG. (*Rising guiltily.*) Yes. Mine.

LUCETTE. (*With disgust.*) He admits it! Oh, the heartless beast!

BOIS D'ENG. Please . . . Lucette . . .

(LUCETTE *crosses to below the chaise longue.*)

LUCETTE. (*With a grand gesture and a bitter smile.*) Very well. I know exactly what I have to do.

BOIS D'ENG. What . . . ?

LUCETTE. (*Opens her bag and fumbles in it.*) I promised you . . .

BOIS D'ENG. I can't remember what you promised me.

(*She puts her bag on the table and takes out a revolver.*)

LUCETTE. (*Strangled voice.*) You wanted it this way.

(*Puts the revolver to her temple.*) Goodbye, my darling. Be happy. With her last breath poor Lucette . . . Blesses you both!

(BOIS D'ENGHIEN *rushes to the* L. *of* LUCETTE, *and struggles with her.*)

BOIS D'ENG. Lucette . . . Don't be ridiculous. Now, Lucette! Lucette, for God's sake!

LUCETTE. (*Struggling.*) Leave me alone . . . ! Will you . . . Leave me alone!

BOIS D'ENG. (*Trying to disarm her and calm her at the same time.*) Lucette, I beg you. Please. Anyway it'd be awfully bad manners . . . in someone else's house.

LUCETTE. (*Bitter laugh.*) Manners! I'm past caring about manners.

BOIS D'ENG. (*Driven mad—holding her all the time.*) But listen . . . You've got to listen to me! You'll understand when I've told you all about it! And how can I tell you if you kill yourself . . . in the middle of the conversation? (LUCETTE *crosses* D. S. *Having freed herself.*) What've you got to say? (BOIS D'ENGHIEN *crosses* D. S. *level with her. Quickly.*) Give me that revolver!

LUCETTE. No . . . tell me first.

B. DUVERGER. (*Offstage.*) Bois d'Enghien! Bois d'Enghien!

(BOIS D'ENGHIEN *crosses* U. S. *to door.*)

BOIS D'ENG. I'm in here! (*He stops.*) Oh my God. Oh my God. (*He crosses* D. R. *a little.*) Don't do anything till I get back . . . (*He exits* U. S. C. *and off* R. LUCETTE *crosses* U. S. *to the door and then turns.*)

LUCETTE. It's stifling in here! (*She pulls the trigger of the revolver—and a fan pops out. She fans herself with it, crossing to* D. S. *of the chaise longue. Aside.*) You're not married yet, my fine little fellow . . . (*She closes the fan and puts the revolver back in the bag.*)

BOIS D'ENG. (*Shouting through the door.*) Yes. I'm coming! Insensitive lot! (LUCETTE *crosses to above the table by the chaise longue as* BOIS D'ENGHIEN *enters* U. S. C. *and stays there, striking an attitude.*) Please, darling! Be brave. Try and behave well . . . for the sake of our great love . . .

LUCETTE. Our great love! (*She throws herself face downwards on the chaise longue.*) Does it still exist?

BOIS D'ENG. (*Crossing to above the chaise longue, and sinking onto his knees.*) What on earth do you mean . . . Does it still exist . . . ?

LUCETTE. (*Sobs of grief.*) Aren't you getting married?

BOIS D'ENG. Whatever's that got to do with it? Does my right hand have to know what my left hand's doing? One of them can be married . . . while the other's making love to you in the afternoons . . . (LUCETTE *kneels on the chaise longue.*)

LUCETTE. (*In a dreamy voice.*) Honestly . . . ? We'll be together sometimes. In the afternoons . . . ?

(BOIS D'ENGHIEN *rises.*)

BOIS D'ENG. (*Trying to sound convincing.*) I solemnly swear to you! Before whatever Gods there may be . . .

LUCETTE. (*Aside.*) He's giving a lovely performance!

(BOIS D'ENGHIEN *takes a pace* D. S.)

BOIS D'ENG. (*Aside.*) She's fallen for it! (*He crosses to the chaise longue and sits on the* U. S. *end of it.*) My Lulu . . .

(LUCETTE *kneels at the* D. S. *end of the chaise longue and pushes* BOIS D'ENGHIEN'S *face down across her lap.*)

LUCETTE. My Ferny . . . Do you love me?
BOIS D'ENG. Desperately!
LUCETTE. Go on telling me, darling! (*She straightens*

up, still on her knees. With her right hand she feels the bouquet of wild flowers. Aside.) That's a good idea! It's really too mean! I'll do it! (*She puts her arms round* BOIS D'ENGHIEN'S *neck. He has his arms round her waist.*) Darling? Can you remember the countryside . . . ?

BOIS D'ENG. (*Trying hard.*) I think I can . . .

(LUCETTE *takes an ear of corn from the bouquet.*)

LUCETTE. When we rolled together in the cornfield . . . like a couple of school children . . .

BOIS D'ENG. (*Aside.*) I knew this was coming . . . "The blue sky . . . The little birds twittering . . ."

LUCETTE. The blue sky . . . The little birds twittering . . .

BOIS D'ENG. (*Aside.*) What did I tell you?

LUCETTE. . . . The wind whispered in the cornfield and I took a great ear of corn and . . . stuffed it down your neck!

(*As* BOIS D'ENGHIEN *listens to her, his head bent forward—she stuffs the ear of corn down his neck.*)

BOIS D'ENG. (*Struggling.*) Careful, darling! What're you doing?

LUCETTE. (*Forcing it down.*) And down it went, darling! (*Looks at the audience and winks.*) Down . . . it . . . went!

(BOIS D'ENGHIEN *jumps up and crosses to below table* L.)

BOIS D'ENG. Now that's silly, darling! I can't reach it!

LUCETTE. (*In a sweet little voice.*) Oh dear . . . does it tickle you, darling?

BOIS D'ENG. Of course it tickles me, darling!

(LUCETTE *rises to her knees.*)

LUCETTE. Poor darling . . . (*Business like.*) All right get it out, darling . . .

BOIS D'ENG. (*Struggling desperately to get it out.*) It's all very well to say "Get it out, darling"! How can I get it out? It's crept under my flannel vest, darling.

LUCETTE. Take it off then, darling.

BOIS D'ENG. Are you mad, darling! Undress! In the middle of my engagement party?

(LUCETTE *rises and crosses* U. S. *to shut the doors and then* R. *to shut the door.*)

LUCETTE. Don't worry! We'll lock all the doors . . . They'll think I'm changing . . . and you've gone.

BOIS D'ENG. Oh oh NO No No! (*He crosses* U. S. *and then* D. S. *trying to dislodge the corn.*) Oh, my God, my God, my God! It's tickling me all over!

(LUCETTE *crosses* C.)

LUCETTE. Stop dancing about, darling! Just go behind the screen and look for it!

(BOIS D'ENGHIEN *crosses to the screen* U. L.)

BOIS D'ENG. I can't stand it any longer. You're sure they're all locked?

LUCETTE. Of course they are! (BOIS D'ENGHIEN *goes behind the screen and pulls it around himself.* LUCETTE *makes a triumphant gesture, and says to the audience.*) Got him! (*Tape cue: waltz.*) I must get ready for my performance!

BOIS D'ENG. (*Behind the screen.*) You've gone too far this time.

(LUCETTE *takes off her bodice and dances to the chair above door* D. L. *and puts the bodice on it.*)

LUCETTE. Why've I gone too far, darling? There's an ear of corn tickling you and you're looking for it behind the screen. It all seems part of nature.

BOIS D'ENG. You've got a way of getting nature on your side. (*His coat comes over the screen.*)

LUCETTE. Darling—I don't mind you getting married at all . . . (*She crosses C. and slips her skirt to the floor and dances out of it D. R. on the end of the line, having thrown the skirt over the back of the chaise longue.*)

BOIS D'ENG. I can't reach it! (*His waistcoat comes over the screen.*)

LUCETTE. I'm just longing for our first afternoon tea— in bed! (*She dances to the chaise longue and lies on it— head D. S., feet up on the back of it by the end of the line.*)

BOIS D'ENG. How could it travel so quickly? (*His shirt comes over the screen.*)

LUCETTE. Shall we make it Thursday? You could say you were going to the Dentist . . . (LUCETTE *dances D. R. and turns to look at the screen at the end of the line.*)

BOIS D'ENG. Having to undress at your own engagement party—it's really most embarrassing.

LUCETTE. (*Pirouetting to the table L. and putting U. S. leg on it at the end of the line.*) How are you getting on? You must be getting warm!

BOIS D'ENG. Ah! (*His trousers come over the screen.*)

LUCETTE. Ole! (*She pirouettes D. R. to L. of D. S. end of the chaise longue.*)

BOIS D'ENG. Got you, you little bastard!

LUCETTE. (*Breathing passionately.*) Let me have it!

BOIS D'ENG. What ever for?

LUCETTE. To treasure! It's been near to your heart . . .

BOIS D'ENG. That's not where I found it at all . . .

LUCETTE. Let me have it all the same.

(BOIS D'ENGHIEN *crosses R. to above* LUCETTE. *He is dressed in his flannel underwear, and holding an ear of corn.*)

Bois d'Eng. All right. Here you are.

Lucette. (*Taking* Bois d'Enghien's *hand as he offers her the corn, and pulling him towards her.*) How beautiful you look like that!

Bois d'Eng. (*Flattered.*) Do I really?

(Lucette *pulls* Bois d'Enghien's *other hand round her.*)

Lucette. He's beautiful! My God, he's beautiful!

Bois d'Eng. Well . . . Perhaps a little beautiful. (*Looks around.*)

Lucette. And when I think . . . When I think all that was going to be taken from me. That warmth! That flesh! That flannel! Without that I couldn't live . . . without you! (*She sits on the chaise longue and pulls* Bois d'Enghien *across her lap, face downwards, facing the audience.*) Oh my Ferny. How I love you . . . How I *love* you! (*Shouts.*) I LOVE YOU! How I love you! (*She rings the electric bell on the table beside her with her right hand.*)

Bois d'Eng. (*On his knees, held by the neck . . . he loses his head.*) Don't answer that 'phone! Keep quiet . . . keep very quiet! (*As he says this,* Lucette *continues to shout.*)

Voice Outside. What's going on? Open the door!

Bois d'Eng. They can't come in. Keep quiet! Keep very quiet!

(*Enter* Marceline u. s. c. *She crosses to* u. s. r. *chaise longue,* De Fontanet *following her and crossing to* u. s. l. *of her.*)

Everyone. Oh!

(*Enter the* Baroness *and crosses* c. Vivianne *enters* u. s. c. *and crosses to* d. r. *of table* l. De Chenneviette *enters and crosses to* d. r. *of* Marceline.)

Bois d'Eng. Don't come in. Please . . . don't come in . . .

B. Duverger. Horror! (*Clasps* Vivianne *to her.*) Horror! Horror! In his flannel vest!

Lucette. (*As if coming out of a dream.*) Never! Never! We've never never made love like that before . . .

(Bois d'Enghien *rises and crosses to* R. *of the* Baroness.)

Bois d'Eng. *What* did she say?

Everyone. Scandalous!

B. Duverger. In my house! Leave at once, M'sieur! (*The* Baroness *takes* Vivianne L. *to below table.*) It's all over!

Bois d'Eng. But Madame, I can easily explain.

(*The* General *enters* U. S. C. *and crosses* R. *to* Bois d'Enghien.)

General. And tomorrow morning at the dawning. I kill you . . .

Bois d'Eng. (*Desperate.*) Oh my God!

CURTAIN

ACT THREE

SCENE: BOIS D'ENGHIEN'S *apartment: The Stage is divided into two parts. The Left part which takes up three-quarters of the Stage is in the second floor hall landing of a new house. Backstage is a very elegant, practical staircase. Coming up from below the Stage and continuing from Left to Right from Stage level. Against the Centre of the banister rail—of the well of the staircase—is a bench* D. S. L. *the front door of* BOIS D'ENGHIEN'S *apartment. It has an electric bell.* U. S. *of the front door, against the wall, is a "Hamlet" chair, upholstered in the same material as the banquette.* D. S. R. *in the wall flat which cuts the set in two, and opposite his front door, is the door to* BOIS D'ENGHIEN'S *dressing room. The door opens into the dressing room, being hinged on its Upstage edge.*

The Right part of the set is the dressing room. In the Right wall is a window opening inwards. Backstage R. *is a swing door which opens onto a corridor— which in turn, although this is not seen—leads to the rest of the apartment and ends on the opposite side of the wash-stand (with practical taps), bearing all the usual toilet utensils; bottles, brushes, combs, sponges, tooth brushes and glasses, towels etc.* D. S. R. *a chair with folded men's clothes on it. Above it an armchair. Between the armchair and the window (on the wall) is a clothes hook on which is hanging a woman's dressing gown, on the floor by it a pair of women's slippers. Against the partition wall is a triple hat stand. The front door and the dressing room door are self locking, and have to be opened with keys.*

108

At the rise of the Curtain, JEAN *is in the dressing room,
standing near the armchair, cleaning his master's
boots. He is holding a boot with one hand, and
polishing it with a duster with the other.*

JEAN. (*Polishing away.*) Very odd . . . ! Ten o'clock
in the morning and he's not back. I'm not all that clean
living myself . . . (*Enter* FLOWER BOY U. S. C. *who
crosses to door* D. L. *He is carrying a large basket of
flowers.*) . . . but if you're engaged, I do think you
should spend the night in your own home . . . (*He
breathes on the boot to bring up the shine.*) Or at least
with your fiancee . . . ! (*The* FLOWER BOY *rings the
DOOR BELL.* JEAN *puts the shoes down in front of the
armchair.*) Who's that? Can't be the master, he's got his
key. (*He puts brush and polish down on the armchair.*) If
you think I'm going all the way round the apartment to
the front door just to open it for him . . . (JEAN *opens
the door to the landing.*) Yes, what is it?

(FLOWER BOY *crosses to landing door* D. R.)

FLOWER BOY. Excuse me! The Brugnot wedding . . . ?
JEAN. (*Bad humouredly.*) Eh? No, it's upstairs on the
third floor!
FLOWER BOY. The concierge said it was the second.
JEAN. Yes, well, it's between the two—on the little half
landing.
FLOWER BOY. Sorry to have troubled you.

(FLOWER BOY *crosses* L. C. *and exits upstairs.* JEAN *shuts
the door and crosses to the armchair.*)

JEAN. It wears you out. That's the sixth one this morning for the Brugnot wedding! If this goes on I'll put a
notice on the door—"not here, it's upstairs!"

(*He removes the shoes and the polishing things and puts*

them under the armchair. BOIS D'ENGHIEN *enters*
U. S. C. *and crosses to doors* L. *He is in evening dress,*
with a cloak and a dejected expression, his tie
crooked, and his shirt crumpled.)

BOIS D'ENG. What a night! (*He rings* L. *for a long*
time.)

(JEAN *crosses to the landing door and opens it.*)

JEAN. Another one for the Brugnot wedding! (*Opens*
the door.) Not here, upstairs!
BOIS D'ENG. What?
JEAN. You, M'sieur! It can't be you, sir?

(BOIS D'ENGHIEN *crosses* R. *to the landing door and*
crosses R. *below* JEAN.)

BOIS D'ENG. Yes it can.

(JEAN *takes* BOIS D'ENGHIEN'S *hat and cane.*)

JEAN. Oh sir . . . Ten o'clock in the morning after
your engagement party. Now is that the right way to behave, M'sieur?
BOIS D'ENG. (*As he removes his coat and* JEAN *takes*
it.) Oh, Jean! Just leave me in peace.
JEAN. Yes, M'sieur.
BOIS D'ENG. It's entirely due to you that I spent a
dreadful night in a hotel.
JEAN. In a hotel? Due to *me*, M'sieur?

(BOIS D'ENGHIEN *removes his waistcoat and* JEAN *takes*
it.)

BOIS D'ENG. Certainly. If you'd had the elementary
consideration to be here when I got back last night. But
oh no! I knocked. I rang . . . I practically beat the door
down . . .

JEAN. But, M'sieur, surely you had your key?

BOIS D'ENG. I lost it down someone's back . . . (*He crosses* U. S. *to dressing table.* JEAN *goes to the hat stand with all the clothes.*)

JEAN. *Where* you lost it is no business of mine, sir.

BOIS D'ENG. Look here, Jean . . . Will you please go . . .

JEAN. And fish it up again?

BOIS D'ENG. No! It can stay where it is! Go and find a carpenter and get him to change the lock.

JEAN. At once, sir. (*He crosses to* U. S. R. *door.*)

BOIS D'ENG. (*Pointing to the door leading to the landing.*) Don't go right round the apartment—use that door, it's quicker.

(JEAN *crosses to the inner door.*)

JEAN. Very good, M'sieur. I've left out everything you need to appear clothed, M'sieur . . . and in your right mind . . . (*He exits through the landing door and crosses* U. S. C. *to exit leaving the landing door open.*)

BOIS D'ENG. Get on with it! (BOIS D'ENGHIEN *sits in the armchair* D. R. *and removes his braces.*) The night of August 16th will go down in history! A night to remember! Dear, sweet Lucette. The darling little trouper! A charming girl! (*He rises.*) My name's mud! I'm thrown out of the house! My marriage is off! Bravo Lucette! (*He crosses* U. S. *to hang his trousers on the hat stand and takes off his shirt.*) But I tell you . . . in the end, Virtue triumphs! And to top it all! A sleepless night in a hotel. In full evening dress with no toothbrush. They took me for a waiter on the run.

(*A* COUPLE *enter* U. S. C., *the man first who crosses to* U. L., *the woman stops* C. BOIS D'ENGHIEN *turns on the tap and begins to wash.*)

WOMAN. (*Points to* BOIS D'ENGHIEN'S *door.*) This must be it.

MAN. Do you think so?

WOMAN. People always leave the door open when it's a question of a party.

MAN. I suppose you're right. (*The* MAN *crosses below the* WOMAN *to the landing door* R. C. *and pushes the door further open.*) Funny. It doesn't *look* like a wedding . . .

BOIS D'ENGHIEN. (*At the wash stand.*) Oh my God . . . !

MAN and WOMAN. Oh! (*They back two paces* L.)

MAN. Pardon us!

WOMAN. A naked man!

BOIS D'ENG. *What do you want?*

MAN. Isn't the Brugnot wedding in here?

BOIS D'ENG. Do I look like a wedding? It's upstairs! And it's very rude to come barging in when people're getting dressed . . . (*He hits the* MAN *with his towel. The* MAN *crosses* L. *below the* WOMAN.)

WOMAN. It's also very rude to leave your door open when you're in an indecent condition!

BOIS D'ENG. I didn't ask you in, did I? It's not a public footpath. I didn't put up a notice . . . "walk up! walk up! See the man in his amazing underpants!" Did I? Get out . . . Go on! Get out! (*He shuts the door in their faces, and crosses to the washbasin* R. *as the couple back.*)

MAN. One of those people you read about in the newspapers . . . (MAN *and* WOMAN *cross* U. L. *to bottom of the stairs* U. L.)

BOIS D'ENG. What a way to behave!

MAN. (*Going upstairs after his wife.*) I told you it was up here.

WOMAN. Anyone can make a mistake!

(WOMAN *takes* MAN's *arm as they exit upstairs.* BOIS D'ENGHIEN *brushes his teeth with toothpowder.*)

BOIS D'ENG. Now I'm doing the concierge's job for him. Why did that idiot leave the door open anyway?

(BOUZIN *enters* U. C. *and crosses* D. L. *to the doors.*)

BOUZIN. Bois d'Enghien . . . second floor. Here it is! (*He RINGS the BELL.*)

BOIS D'ENG. (*Who's just poured out water to clean his teeth.*) Marvellous! The door bell, and Jean's not here. Who'd come round at this unearthly hour? They'll just have to wait . . .

BOUZIN. No one there? (*He RINGS again.*)

BOIS D'ENG. I can't go to the door like this.

BOUZIN. We shall see. (*He puts his finger on the bell—a loud RING.*)

(BOIS D'ENGHIEN *crosses to the landing door and opens it a little.*)

BOIS D'ENG. What . . . who is it . . . ?

(BOUZIN *crosses to landing door, stopping* L. *of it.*)

BOUZIN. M'sieur Bois d'Enghien. It's me!

BOIS D'ENG. Sorry. I'm not at home. (*He starts to shut the door.*)

BOUZIN. This won't take a moment. (*He holds the door open.*) M'sieur Lantery sent me . . .

BOIS D'ENG. I'm undressed . . .

(BOUZIN *goes in the landing door and crosses to the armchair* D. R., *takes off his gloves and puts them on the arm of the chair.*)

BOUZIN. I'm a man of the world, M'sieur.

BOIS D'ENG. Oh all right. Well . . . (*He crosses* D. R. *to* BOUZIN.) What is it?

BOUZIN. I've been told to give you this copy of your marriage settlement, M'sieur. (*He takes the document out of his case.*)

BOIS D'ENG. My marriage settlement? (*He crosses* U. S. *a little and back to* BOUZIN.) Oh very good! Oh ha! Ha! Ha! Oh you've just come at the right moment, you have.

You can . . . you know what you can do with my marriage settlement?

BOUZIN. Please, M'sieur. Don't say it.

BOIS D'ENG. Haven't you heard? It's all off. Look. (*He crosses* U. S. *after tearing up the marriage settlement.*)

BOUZIN. Oh no! (*Tries to pick up the pieces.*) Well, it's your life, M'sieur! I was also told to bring you your account for professional services, including stamp duty . . .

(BOIS D'ENGHIEN *crosses back to the* L. *of* BOUZIN. BOUZIN *rises. The* GENERAL *enters* U. C. *and crosses to the doors* L.)

BOIS D'ENG. Oh marvellous! Oh I like that! Don't you understand? I'm ruined!

BOUZIN. (*Who's been trying to fit the pieces together.*) You may be ruined, but it all costs money.

(*The* GENERAL, *barely concealing his rage, RINGS the BELL.*)

BOIS D'ENG. Now who is it?

BOUZIN. Excuse me, but . . .

(*The* GENERAL *paces to* C. *and back to* L.)

BOIS D'ENG. Yes. Yes. In a moment. Look would you do me a favour? My man's gone out and . . . Could you possibly go to the door?

BOUZIN. Certainly! (*He starts to go to the landing door.*)

BOIS D'ENG. No! That way . . . (*He points to the* U. S. *door and* BOUZIN *crosses to it and exits.*) Take the passage to the right . . . and tell whoever it is, I'm out. (*The* GENERAL *RINGS again.*) What's the matter with everyone today? They're ringing like lunatics!

GENERAL. Caramba! Me ran hacer esperer toda lavida.

(*RINGS again.*)

BOIS D'ENG. (*Laughs.*) Patience!

BOUZIN. (*Offstage.*) I'm coming . . .

GENERAL. Good. Let's see you. (*He bangs on the door.*)

BOUZIN. (*Opening the door and recognizing the* GENERAL.) Ooo no! It's the Last of the Mohicans! (*He retreats rapidly, shutting the door in the* GENERAL'S *face.*)

GENERAL. (*Banging on the door again.*) Poussin! What did he call me? He called me the last of the . . . Poussin! Open up! Abrir! Presto! Idiota!

(BOIS D'ENGHIEN *opens the landing door slightly.*)

BOIS D'ENG. What's going on?

(*The* GENERAL *comes into* BOIS D'ENGHIEN'S *dressing room like a bomb . . . and the latter is pushed out of the way by the door. The* GENERAL *crosses to the armchair* D. R.)

GENERAL. You! It's you! Bueno. Later for you. Now I get Poussin!

(BOIS D'ENGHIEN *shuts the landing door and stays on the* R. *of it.*)

BOIS D'ENG. What do you want him for?

GENERAL. He called me a Mohican! Me . . . ! (*Pause.*) What is a Mohican?

(BOUZIN *enters door* U. S. R. *and crosses to* BOIS D'ENGHIEN.)

BOUZIN. (*Terrified.*) Oo, M'sieur, it's the General! Help! (*He crosses* U. S. *and exits.*)

(*The* GENERAL *follows him.*)

GENERAL. Ha ha! Wait Poussin. Momento Poussin!

Bois d'Eng. (*Trying to get between them.*) You *must* try to stop chasing people.

General. Let me go! I'll see you later . . . (*Rushes off in pursuit.*)

Bouzin. (*Offstage.*) Help! Help!

Bois d'Eng. I'll get complaints from the landlord . . .

Bouzin. (*Offstage.*) Help! Help! (Bouzin *enters door* D. L. *and slams it shut.* Bois d'Enghien *opens the landing door and stands to the* L. *of it.* Bouzin *exits upstairs.*) Don't tell him where I've gone . . . (Flower Boy *starts coming downstairs.*) Don't tell him!

Bois d'Eng. (*Laughing.*) All right!

(Bouzin *collides with the* Flower Boy *who is coming hurriedly down the stairs.* Bouzin *falls, bouncing down the stairs to the bottom on his behind. The* Flower Boy *exits* U. S. C., *and* Bouzin *rushes upstairs out of sight.*)

Flower Boy Why don't you look where you're going?

(*The* General *rushes in* D. L. *and crosses* C.)

General. Where's Poussin?

Bois d'Eng. He just went downstairs . . .

General. Ah I can see you . . . ! Wait Poussin . . . I see you with my own eyes . . . So . . . I am a Mohican. Am I? Hasta la Muerte . . .

(*He exits* U. S. C. Bouzin *appears at the top of the stairs as* Bois d'Enghien *follows the* General U. S. *and calls after him.*)

Bois d'Eng. Run . . . You might even catch him!

Bouzin. Pst! Pst! (Bois d'Enghien *looks all around him to see where the noise is coming from. Then he turns to* Bouzin *and crosses* U. S. *a little.*) Has he gone . . . ?

Bois d'Eng. (*Laughing.*) It's all right. He's running after you!

(BOUZIN *makes for the landing door of the dressing room.*)

BOUZIN. Ooh . . . I thought he had me that time!

(*He crosses* R. *and sits in the armchair.* BOIS D'ENGHIEN *crosses to the landing door.*)

BOIS D'ENG. (*Shutting the door.*) You must've broken the record for the course.

BOUZIN. I can't spend all my life on the trot. What's the matter with the cannibal? I'll end up a nervous wreck. What have I got that sets him off every time he sees me?

(BOIS D'ENGHIEN *crosses to the* L. *of* BOUZIN *and pretends to be serious.*)

BOIS D'ENG. Do you mean you don't know what sets him off?

BOUZIN. That's what I keep asking myself.

BOIS D'ENG. It's just the fact that you went to bed with Lucette Gautier.

BOUZIN. (*Rises and protests loudly.*) Me? I never even had tea with her! (*Misunderstanding* BOIS D'ENGHIEN'S *smile.*) I give you my word of honour!

BOIS D'ENG. Oh really?

BOUZIN. Yes! And if she's spreading that story around I tell you quite frankly—she's boasting! I suppose she could fancy me, though she's never said, and I'm going about in peril of my life, just so that Lucette Gautier can impress her friends.

BOIS D'ENG. It's not fair!

(*Enter* LUCETTE U. S. C. *and crosses* D. C.)

BOUZIN. It's not! You must explain to the General he's made a mistake, a terrible mistake! If this goes on I won't have much longer to live.

Bois d'Eng. Calm down. I'll have a word with him.

Lucette. (*Taking a deep breath.*) Here we go! I've got my irresistible hat on! (*She crosses to door* D. L. *and RINGS the bell.*)

Bois d'Eng. (*At the SOUND of the bell.*) Not again! (Bouzin *crosses* D. S. *of dressing table and takes a bottle ready to strike.*) Oh my dear Bouzin. Would you just mind . . . ?

Bouzin. I'm not an idiot! It might be the artillery . . .

(Lucette *RINGS again.*)

Bois d'Eng. I can't go to the door like this!

Lucette. I'll use the key he put down my corset. It must have been put there for a reason. (*She crosses* R. *to landing door.*)

Bois d'Eng. Go on, Bouzin. Do me a favour.

Bouzin. (*Determined.*) Absolutely not! (Lucette *puts the key in the landing door.*) The Generals are coming! (*He puts the bottle back on the dressing table and hides with* Bois d'Enghien *behind the curtains on the window.*)

Lucette. (*Coming in cold and determined.*) It's me!

Bouzin. Lucette Gautier!

Bois d'Eng. You!

Lucette. Yes . . . me! (*Bangs the door shut.*)

(Bois d'Enghien *crosses to the armchair.*)

Bois d'Eng. The ice cold nerve!

Lucette. I must speak to you.

Bouzin. (*Taking one pace in.*) To me!

Lucette. (*Shrugs.*) Not to you . . . (*To* Bois d'Enghien.) To you! (*To* Bouzin.) Please leave us, M'sieur Bouzin.

(Bouzin *crosses to door* U. S. R.)

Bois d'Eng. Don't bother. We have nothing to say to each other.

LUCETTE. (*Firmly.*) I must speak to you. Leave us, M'sieur Bouzin!

BOIS D'ENG. (*Scornful.*) Very well. Will you wait, M'sieur Bouzin? I'll call you when Madame has had her say . . .

BOUZIN. All right. (*He crosses to door U. S. R.*) Yes. She's certainly eyeing me! (*He exits U. S. R.*)

BOIS D'ENG. (*With suppressed fury.*) What do you want now?

LUCETTE. I came . . . (*Nervously as he stares coldly at her.*) to bring your key back. (*She gives the key to* BOIS D'ENGHIEN *who puts it on the dressing table.*)

BOIS D'ENG. Very well. (*He crosses level with* LUCETTE.) I don't imagine there's anything else . . .

LUCETTE. Yes there is. (*Throws her arms round him.*) Help me unhook my dress, darling!

(BOIS D'ENGHIEN *puts* LUCETTE *to his* R.)

BOIS D'ENG. As far as I'm concerned you can stay hooked up for ever!

LUCETTE. Don't be ridiculous, I love you.

BOIS D'ENG. I may have been stupid for a long time . . . But there are limits . . . (*He takes a step away from* LUCETTE.) Do you honestly think you can break up my marriage? Make me look a complete utter imbecile and then come back and say "I love you" and I'll say "thank you, Lulu darling" and trot back to my kennel? (LUCETTE *collapses into the armchair* R.)

LUCETTE. The ingratitude!

(BOIS D'ENGHIEN *takes a step towards* LUCETTE.)

BOIS D'ENG. Let me tell you. I'm fed to the eyeballs with you loving me. I'm sick to death of you loving me! I don't even like you loving me! And just to prove it . . . Look . . . (*He opens the landing door.*) Is there anything keeping you?

(LUCETTE *rises*.)

LUCETTE. You're showing *me* the door! Me . . . Me, Lucette Gautier?

BOIS D'ENG. You're not Sarah Bernhardt! It's all over. Finished. Broken off. Goodbye. Goodbye.

LUCETTE. Once is quite enough. (*She goes.* BOIS D'ENG-HIEN *shuts the door on her, but* LUCETTE *stops the door from shutting, and comes back into the room.*) I'm warning you. One step outside that door—and I'll be gone for ever!

BOIS D'ENG. Is that a promise!

LUCETTE. Yes! (*Just as before,* LUCETTE *goes and comes back when he tries to shut the door.*) Think it over!

BOIS D'ENG. I have!

LUCETTE. I'll never come back. Not if you go down on your hands and knees and wriggle under my bedroom door!

BOIS D'ENG. I wouldn't attempt it.

LUCETTE. Very well then! (*She goes.* BOIS D'ENGHIEN *shuts the door on her. She tries to come back as before.*) But you know— (*She finds the door closed.*) Fernand! (*Banging on the door.*) Will you open the door?

BOIS D'ENG. (*In his room.*) No!

LUCETTE. (*Through the door.*) Think what you're doing! (*She crosses to the banquette* C. *and sits on it.*) I've made you the envy of Cabinet Ministers. You'll suffer horribly . . .

BOIS D'ENG. I'll try and be brave. (*He unhooks her dressing gown, rolls it up, opens the landing door and throws it at her feet.*) You can take back your dressing gown! (*He shuts the door and gets her slippers.*)

LUCETTE. Oh!

BOIS D'ENG. (*Opening the door again.*) And your bed-room slippers! (*Shuts the door again.* LUCETTE *rises.*)

LUCETTE. Very well then! You be like that! And when I'm stretched out on a marble slab like some exquisite fish everyone'll know who's responsible . . .

BOIS D'ENG. Responsible for what?

(LUCETTE *crosses* D. L.)

LUCETTE. (*Taking the revolver out of her muff.*) You remember my little revolver? It's the only friend I've got left.

(BOIS D'ENGHIEN *rushes to the door and pulls it open.*)

BOIS D'ENG. Stop that . . . (*Throws himself on* LUCETTE.) Will you give me that!

LUCETTE. I'll leave it to you in my will!

BOIS D'ENG. (*Trying to grab the revolver as they struggle.*) Don't do it! (*Aside as he holds the hand with the revolver in it.*) Why's that wretched revolver always bringing us together?

LUCETTE. Goodbye! Goodbye! With her last breath, Lucette forgives you!

BOIS D'ENG. Now come along, Lucette. Please! Let me have it!

LUCETTE. I won't!

BOIS D'ENG. You will.

(*He seizes the barrel of the revolver.* LUCETTE *has her hand on the butt. The fan shoots out.* LUCETTE *crosses* U. S. *and back again.*)

LUCETTE. Oh! Oh dear . . .

BOIS D'ENG. A fan! Little Lucette's Jokes and Novelties! Where's your rubber dagger, darling?

LUCETTE. (*Furious, stamping with rage.*) I meant it. It's the thought that counts.

BOIS D'ENG. She even kills herself . . . with a prop left over from last year's pantomime. You must be the biggest ham in the business. Certainly the oldest!

LUCETTE. Did you call me an old ham?

BOIS D'ENG. Yes. I did.

LUCETTE. Then it's over. There's nothing ahead for you in life, Fernand. Don't stop me, I know the way out. (*She starts to exit* U. S. C. *but comes back.*) And another thing —this is Lucette Gautier's positively last appearance! (*She exits* U. S. C.)

BOIS D'ENG. (*Picks up the fan from the banquette.*) Oh dear, oh dear, oh dear. And for once I really believed her. Suicide with that! She must've got it out of a cracker! (*He puts the fan back in the revolver and leaves it on the banquette.*) Peace at last! (*He crosses to his dressing room with* LUCETTE'S *dressing gown and throws it out of the window.*) You forgot your dressing gown! (*He crosses* C. *for the slippers as the landing door slams shut.*) Oh lovely! The door's slammed! (*Shouting and knocking.*) Open up! My God . . . I left the key on the washstand. Jean! No . . . he's gone out. But I can't hang about on the landing like this. (*He crosses* U. S.) Concierge! Concierge!

BOUZIN. (*Appearing timidly* U. S. R. *and closing the windows* R.) You haven't forgotten me, have you, M'sieur Bois d'Enghien . . . He's gone!

BOIS D'ENG. (*Collapses on the banquette.*) Oh my God . . . And to think someone's getting married up there . . .

BOUZIN. Oh well, I'll come back later.

BOIS D'ENG. I'll ring. Bouzin might hear. (*He rings endlessly.*)

BOUZIN. (*Who was about to open the door, is terrified.*) There's Hiawatha's ring! And there's no one here to protect me!

BOIS D'ENG. (*Ringing madly.*) He's not coming . . . He's afraid to come . . . what a delightful situation! Out on the landing in my underpants! (BOUZIN *starts to exit* U. S. C.) NO! Someone's coming up. (*He dashes to the staircase which goes upstairs, runs up, disappears and emerges again in a panic.*) It's the wedding! The wedding's coming down. Oh my God! I'm surrounded!

(*He crosses* D. S. L. *and tries to disappear into the door-*

way L. *The wedding party comes clattering down the stairs—all talking at once. It consists of ten guests coming down the stairs in pairs. They stop and see* BOIS D'ENGHIEN *as the bride and her father reach* R. C. *by the landing door. The bride's father sees him first. They all stop talking and stare at him before* BOIS D'ENGHIEN *says the line marked 3 then ad lib as before with horror, and exit* U. S. C.)

FATHER-IN-LAW. Come along, everyone. Hurry up . . . Pick your feet up then.

BRIDE. We've got heaps of time.

SON-IN-LAW. We've got to be there at 11 . . .

EVERYONE. (*Seeing* BOIS D'ENGHIEN.) Oh!

BOIS D'ENG. (*3.*) (*Trying to carry it off with a brave smile.*) Please accept . . . my best wishes for your f it⁺ ᵉ happiness.

EVERYONE. (*Throwing up their hands.*) What a revolting object!

FATHER-IN-LAW. A person in underpants!

SON-IN-LAW. I shall lodge a complaint!

BROTHER-IN-LAW. Get the Concierge!

BRIDE. Have it taken away!

BOIS D'ENG. (*By making a lot of little bows he circles round to the* L.) Ladies and Gentlemen. On this no doubt happy occasion . . .

EVERYONE. Please hide yourself, sir. What a revolting object . . . Indecent exposure!

BOIS D'ENG. (*Desperate.*) I can't understand it. My charm's not working. (*Enter the* GENERAL U. S. C. BOIS D'ENGHIEN *sees him.*) Good . . . the General.

(*The* GENERAL *crosses* L. *to* U. S. C. *of* BOIS D'ENGHIEN *and taps his shoulder with his cane.*)

GENERAL. Bodyguard . . . In the underdrawers!

BOIS D'ENG. He's all I need.

GENERAL. Why you in the underdrawers . . . ?

(BOIS D'ENGHIEN *crosses* R. *to the landing door.*)

BOIS D'ENG. Because the door slammed . . . behind my back!

GENERAL (*Laughing.*) Very funny! Mucho comico!

BOIS D'ENG. It's not mucho comico for me . . .

(*The* GENERAL *crosses* L.)

GENERAL. And Poussin. You know I ran after Poussin?

BOIS D'ENG. I don't really care. Anyway you didn't catch him . . .

GENERAL. Oh yes. I got my boot to him . . . but he wasn't Poussin! Clever of him. He changed himself.

BOIS D'ENG. Oh . . .

GENERAL. But I will catch him . . . when he's himself.

(BOIS D'ENGHIEN *crosses* C.)

BOIS D'ENG. What do you want me to do about it?

(*The* GENERAL *crosses to the* L. *of* BOIS D'ENGHIEN *and takes him by the arm* D. C.)

GENERAL. Nothing! I came to attack you about something else.

BOIS D'ENG. About what?

GENERAL. About you!

BOIS D'ENG. Later on. At the moment I've got other things on my mind. (*He crosses* R. *to the landing door.*)

GENERAL. But nothing on the under-neath!

BOIS D'ENG. (*Aside.*) That might sound funny in Mexican. (*Aloud.*) I've been shut out of my rooms.

GENERAL. It doesn't matter.

BOIS D'ENG. What?

GENERAL. It's a bacatil. We can talk out here.

BOIS D'ENG. But you don't understand. (*He crosses* U. C. *then upstairs* U. L.) Somebody's coming . . .

GENERAL. Now where's he got to? Bodyguard! Bodyguard!

BOIS D'ENG. (*From the floor above.*) Later! Later!

GENERAL. The man can't keep stopping still. (*A* MAN *enters* U. C. *and crosses up the stairs* U. L.) Buenos dias! What's he doing up there? Bodyguard! (*He puts one knee on the banquette and calls upstairs.*) Bodyguard! Bueno Bodyguard! (*With an enormous yell.*) Bo . . . dy . . . guard!

BOIS D'ENG. (*From above, yells.*) *What?*

GENERAL. Come down here!

(BOIS D'ENGHIEN *comes downstairs and crosses to the landing door.*)

BOIS D'ENG. Well all right then. Here I am . . .

(*The* GENERAL *gets off the banquette.*)

GENERAL. Bueno! What's the matter with you, Bodyguard? Why you like shooting in and out the bolt?

BOIS D'ENG. Because I don't want to present myself to the world at large without my trousers on. (*Pulls at the door.*) This bloody door! Have you got anything useful on you? A jemmy?

GENERAL. A jemmy?

BOIS D'ENG. Yes.

GENERAL. A precious jemmy?

(BOIS D'ENGHIEN *crosses to the* R. *of the* GENERAL.)

BOIS D'ENG. Oh please! Don't try any sort of joke. What're you here for, anyway?

GENERAL. I came to kill you—but now I can't kill you.

(BOIS D'ENGHIEN *crosses to the landing door.*)

BOIS D'ENGHIEN. (*Angry.*) I suppose that's all to the good.

GENERAL. I need you alive, Bodyguard, and kicking. I met Lucette down with the stairs. She says she'll never sleep me unless I make you sleep her once again.

BOIS D'ENG. What?

GENERAL. So, Bodyguard—you will sleep Lucette again. Tonight!

BOIS D'ENG. Never!

GENERAL. Attention, Bodyguard!

BOIS D'ENG. Not tonight, not any night.

GENERAL. I have to kill you all over again!

(BOIS D'ENGHIEN *crosses to below the* GENERAL *to* D. L. *and turns to him.*)

BOIS D'ENG. The man's a positive menace! Be reasonable! One moment you try to kill me because I'm Lucette's lover. Now you're going to kill me because I'm not. Make up your mind—what do you want exactly?

GENERAL. Stupido! I want Lucette!

(BOIS D'ENGHIEN *crosses to the* L. *of the* GENERAL.)

BOIS D'ENG. Simple—go and tell her I said she's a cold fish in bed!

GENERAL. What? She eat the fish in bed?

BOIS D'ENG. No, no. In bed she's cold—brr!

GENERAL. Oh!

BOIS D'ENG. It's not true, but it's a question of vanity. Her pride will be hurt and she'll go to bed with you just to prove she's hot stuff!

GENERAL. Bueno! Ferny! Oh muchas gracias. Mi amigo —I go to Lucette . . . Adios, Ferny! Hasta la vista! Hunt the trousers. Hot stuffo!

(*Exit the* GENERAL U. S. C. BOIS D'ENGHIEN *sits on the banquette.*)

BOIS D'ENG. There's nothing worse than a Mexican sex maniac.

(BOUZIN *enters door* U. R. *and crosses to the landing door, opens it and crosses in to the landing.*)

BOUZIN. It seems to have gone quiet . . . And I'm not planning to spend the night here.

BOIS D'ENG. (*Seeing* BOUZIN *come out* R. *onto the landing, crosses to* L. *of* BOUZIN.) Don't shut that door!

BOUZIN. (*Shuts the door, startled.*) What?

BOIS D'ENG. Fathead! I told you not to shut it!

BOUZIN. It was too quick for me.

(BOIS D'ENGHIEN *crosses* D. L. *then* U. S., *then back to door* D. L.)

BOIS D'ENG. Charming! So I'm still shut out!

BOUZIN. (*Laughs.*) You haven't got any trousers on! What's the motive behind that, then?

BOIS D'ENG. Do you think I make a habit of it?

BOUZIN. It looks very funny . . .

BOIS D'ENG. Oh ha! Ha! Ha! Oh enjoy the joke. Life's all very entertaining—for those in trousers. You miserable cretin! (*He sits* D. L. *on the pistol.*) Oh! (*Sees the pistol and says aside.*) I think I have hit on a rather ruthless scheme. (*He crosses slowly to the* L. *of* BOUZIN. *Very friendly.*) Bouzin, my dear fellow. . . .

BOUZIN. Yes, M'sieur Bois d'Enghien?

BOIS D'ENG. Could you do me the most enormous favour?

BOUZIN. Could I . . . do you a favour?

BOIS D'ENG. Give me your trousers!

BOUZIN. (*Smiling.*) You're out of your mind!

BOIS D'ENG. Yes! Unhinged! Your trousers or your life! (*Points the revolver at* BOUZIN.)

BOUZIN. (*Terrified, moving against the far end of the partition.*) Don't shoot me—spare me! M'sieur Bois d'Enghien!

BOIS D'ENG. Get 'em off!

BOUZIN. Yes of course. Naturally, M'sieur Bois d'Enghien. It's a pleasure. (*He puts his umbrella on* BOIS D'ENGHIEN'S *arm, his briefcase against the door. He pushes* BOIS D'ENGHIEN'S *arm* r. s. *to turn the revolver away from him and takes off his shoes and trousers.*) Oh dear. Oh dear. What a state of affairs! Having to strip off on the staircase of a totally strange house.

BOIS D'ENG. Hurry up! (BOUZIN *gives him his trousers.*) Thank you very much. Now your jacket . . . (*Points the revolver again.*)

BOUZIN. But what're you leaving me with?

BOIS D'ENG. Your waistcoat. Jacket! (BOUZIN *gives it to him.*) Thank you, M'sieur Bouzin.

(BOUZIN *snatches his umbrella back.* BOIS D'ENGHIEN *crosses to the banquette and sits, putting the revolver down on his* R. BOUZIN *puts on his shoes, picks up his briefcase and covers himself with his hat.*)

BOUZIN. Why did I ever set foot in this place? (BOIS D'ENGHIEN *rises and stands with his back to the audience trying to put on the trousers which are much too small. He crosses* D. L. *and stands facing* D. L. *having done up the trousers.* BOUZIN *crosses to* U. S. C. *exit, and then stops on seeing the revolver. Takes it. He tips his hat over his eyes, like a gangster and crosses* D. L. *to* BOIS D'ENGHIEN.) M'sieur Bois d'Enghien . . . ?

BOIS D'ENG. My dear chap?

BOUZIN. Hand 'em over!

(BOIS D'ENGHIEN *turns to* BOUZIN.)

BOIS D'ENG. What?

BOUZIN. My trousers or your life! (BOIS D'ENGHIEN *finishes dressing.*) I'm not joking. Give me my trousers or I *fire*. I fire . . .

(BOIS D'ENGHIEN *crosses* C. *to below* BOUZIN.)

BOIS D'ENG. Fire away, old fellow.

Bouzin. (*Trying vainly to fire*) What . . . ?

Bois d'Eng. Only not like that. Like this . . . (*He pulls the trigger while* Bouzin *is still holding the gun. The fan pops out.*) You just don't know how to handle firearms.

Bouzin. It's not fair!

(Bois d'Enghien *takes the revolver and puts it in his trouser pocket, and crosses to the landing door.*)

Bois d'Eng. I'm sorry, Bouzin.

Concierge. (*Offstage.*) This way. Gentlemen . . .

(Bouzin *looks* u. s. *and then crosses upstairs.*)

Bouzin. M'sieur! We're not alone! Please help me! Tell them I didn't mean it and send up some trousers or a jacket or something . . .

Bois d'Eng. It's nice to feel dressed—even as Bouzin.

(*The* Concierge *followed by* Two Policemen *enter* u. s. c. *and then cross to stairs* u. l.)

Concierge. This way, gentlemen!

(Bois d'Enghien *crosses to the banquette.*)

Bois d'Eng. The Police! What do you want . . . ?

(*The* Policemen *and* Concierge *go upstairs.*)

Concierge. There's been a naked man prancing about on my staircase . . .

Bois d'Eng. A naked man! (*Aside.*) Oh unfortunate Bouzin! (*Aloud.*) But, gentlemen, I haven't seen anything of the sort . . .

Concierge. (*On the first step of the staircase.*) We received a complaint! From the Brugnot wedding. I went for the Police in person. Exposing himself on a wedding day! Most uncalled for! There's only five floors. He can't be higher than the fifth.

(*The* CONCIERGE *follows the* POLICE *upstairs, calling after them.*)

BOIS D'ENG. Oh unfortunate Bouzin. (*He crosses to the landing door.*) He'll never get away with it.

(*Enter* VIVIANNE U. S. C. *followed by the* FRAULEIN. VIVIANNE *is holding a roll of music.*)

VIVIANNE. Dieser weg, Fraulein.
FRAULEIN. Er geht schon.

(VIVIANNE *crosses to* U. S. L. *of* BOIS D'ENGHIEN, FRAULEIN *to* L. C.)

BOIS D'ENG. Vivianne! You're not here!
VIVIANNE. I *am* here!
BOIS D'ENG. But after . . . what's happened!
VIVIANNE. What's happened! I know now . . . you're the husband of my dreams . . .
BOIS D'ENG. Really? (*Aside.*) Peculiar dreams . . .
FRAULEIN. Wer ist dieser Herr?

(VIVIANNE *crosses to* U. R. *of* FRAULEIN.)

VIVIANNE. Ja! Ja! (*Introducing them,* BOIS D'ENGHIEN *crosses to* C.) My governess, Fraulein Fitzenspiegel . . . Signor Caporelli.

(BOIS D'ENGHIEN *and* FRAULEIN *bow to each other.*)

BOIS D'ENG. (*Amazed.*) What?
FRAULEIN. (*Nodding to* BOIS D'ENGHIEN.) Oh ja! Signor Caporelli.

BOIS D'ENG. What're you talking about?

VIVIANNE. (*To* BOIS D'ENGHIEN.) Do you think she'd've brought me to see you? I said you were my singing teacher.

BOIS D'ENG. But she'll find out!

VIVIANNE. Why? She can't understand a word we say. (*She smiles at the* FRAULEIN *who smiles back.* BOIS D'ENGHIEN *smiles too.*)

FRAULEIN. (*Stops smiling.*) Warum, bleiben wir auf der Trappen?

BOIS D'ENG. (*Laughs.*) What's she talking about?

(VIVIANNE *takes a pace to the* L. *smiling at the* FRAULEIN.)

VIVIANNE. (*Laughs.*) She wonders why we stay on the staircase. (*She turns to take* BOIS D'ENGHIEN R. *The* FRAULEIN *turns* D. L. *to the door.*) Let's go into your bachelor apartment . . .

BOIS D'ENG. Can't be done. The door's shut. Someone's gone for a key.

VIVIANNE. But my singing lesson . . .

BOIS D'ENG. Tell her . . . all great teachers give their singing lessons on the stairs. More room for the high notes . . .

VIVIANNE. Bright idea. (*To* FRAULEIN.) Signor Caporelli gibt immer seinen Gesangstuden auf der Trappen.

FRAULEIN. (*Surprised.*) Nein! (*She goes* D. L. *and sits.*)

VIVIANNE. Ja! (*To* BOIS D'ENGHIEN.) I suppose you've had hundreds of women . . . ?

BOIS D'ENG. Well, as a matter of fact. . . .

VIVIANNE. Tell me, it's so exciting.

BOIS D'ENG. A couple of hundred, actually.

VIVIANNE. And women have actually killed themselves for you?

BOIS D'ENG. Funny you should say that—one tried it this afternoon. Here's her little revolver. I had to take it off her before she did herself a permanent injury.

VIVIANNE. No more talking.

BOIS D'ENG. Why?

VIVIANNE. Mama will be here in a minute.

BOIS D'ENG. Your Mother here? What on earth's she going to say?

VIVIANNE. We can't talk about that now.

BOIS D'ENG. Why not?

VIVIANNE. We're having a singing lesson. If you've something to say—sing it!

BOIS D'ENG. What!

VIVIANNE. Then Fraulein won't get suspicious. Here, take this . . . (*She gives the sheet music of* Carmen *first to the* FRAULEIN *and then to* BOIS D'ENGHIEN.) . . . And now—what was it you were singing?

(*Duet for* VIVIANNE *and* BOIS D'ENGHIEN *to the tune of the duet from* Carmen.)

BOIS D'ENG.
  If Mama comes up here
  She'll think the worst

VIVIANNE.
  Exactly so!
  And that is why
  I left a note
  To say I was in your bachelor apartment.

BOIS D'ENG. (*On one note.*)
  Are you out of your mind?

FRAULEIN. (*Speaks.*) Ah sehr schön! Carmen!

BOIS D'ENG. (*Speaks.*) Is it? Oh yes, of course. Carmen! Wunderbar!

VIVIANNE. (*Resumes song.*)
  She'll think
  That you and I've
  Been making love all afternoon.

BOIS D'ENG. (*On one note.*)
  She's got an absolutely filthy mind!

VIVIANNE.
   And as my reputation's gone
   She'll get us wed
   As soon as possible.
BOIS D'ENG. (*On one note.*)
   What a cunning machination!
VIVIANNE.
   So I'll be Madame d'Enghien . . .
BOIS D'ENG.
   I really think that would be best!
VIVIANNE.
   You've won my heart
   My Ferny dear . . .
BOIS D'ENG. (*With a great effort to get all the words in.*)
   It only goes to show what you can do
   When you show them your flannel vest!

(FRAULEIN *applauds. The* BARONESS *comes rushing up the stairs* U. S. C.)

B. DUVERGER. Vivianne!
VIVIANNE. Mama!
B. DUVERGER. What are you doing here? Wretched child! (*She crosses to the* R. *of* VIVIANNE *and* BOIS D'ENGHIEN *goes* R. *To the* FRAULEIN.) Aren't you ashamed, Madame—bringing my child to the home of this . . . suburban Casanova!
FRAULEIN. Was meinem sie?
B. DUVERGER. Oh she's always hiding behind that German . . .
BOIS D'ENG. Madame. I have the honour to ask for your daughter's hand back.
B. DUVERGER. Not as long as I live! (*To* VIVIANNE.) Wretched child. You couldn't marry him after that scandal.
VIVIANNE. You're quite wrong. I can and I will.
B. DUVERGER. (*Taking* VIVIANNE *in her arms as if to shield her.*) Him! He's Lucette Gautier's poodle!

Bois d'Eng. I'm not Lucette Gautier's poodle any more!

B. Duverger. But last night . . . !

(Bois d'Enghien *crosses* L. *a little.*)

Bois d'Eng. I was breaking it off.

B. Duverger. Oh yes. In that attire . . .

Bois d'Eng. Exactly! I was trying to say to her "I don't want to keep anything that reminds me of you. Not even the garments you've touched!"

B. Duverger. What?

Bois d'Eng. So . . . suiting the action to the word I started to undress. Two minutes later I'd've rejected that dishonoured vest!

B. Duverger. (*Shocked.*) Oh!

Vivianne. You see, Mama. He's a perfect husband!

B. Duverger. (*Resigned.*) If you'd really be happy . . .

Vivianne. Oh Mama!

(Bois d'Enghien *kisses the* Baroness's *hand.*)

B. Duverger. My son!

Bois d'Enghien. Mother!

(Jean *enters* U. S. C. *with key and starts to cross to the landing door.*)

Vivianne. (*To the* Fraulein.) I'm going to marry him!

Fraulein. Bitte?

Vivianne. Ich werde ihn heiraten!

(Jean *unlocks the door.*)

Fraulein. Signor Caporelli? Gott in Himmel!

Jean. Where's M'sieur vanished to . . . ?

(*He opens the landing door.* Bois d'Enghien *crosses to the landing door and beckons the* Baroness *and* Vivianne *to join him.*)

Bois d'Eng. Jean! You're late! Come in, Mother-in-law . . . (Jean *enters the dressing room and keeps* u. s.) Come in, Vivianne, darling. Come in, Fraulein . . .

(*The* Baroness, Vivianne *and* Fraulein *all cross* r. *At that moment there's a great outcry from upstairs.*)

Everyone. What's going on . . . ?

(*Enter the* Concierge *at the top of the stairs* u. l., *followed by* Bouzin *held by the* Two Policemen. *They are visible to the* Baroness, Vivianne *etc., when they get nearly to the bottom of the stairs at which point the* Baroness *crosses to the armchair and sits down—half fainting, the* Fraulein *kneeling* u. s. *of her and fanning her.* Vivianne, *having at first gone into the dressing room, now stands at the landing door, enjoying the spectacle.*)

Concierge. We got him . . . we chased him across the roof. Nabbed the pervert!
Bois d'Eng. Bouzin!
B. Duverger. The lawyer's clerk. In his unpresentables!
Vivianne. What an appalling sight!
Fraulein. Pchrecklich.
Police. Come along with us.
Bouzin. (*Pulling back.*) Oh M'sieur Bois d'Enghien! Please . . . help me . . .
Bois d'Eng. If I were you, old chap, I'd cover myself up!
Police. Come along now, down to the Station.

(Bouzin *escapes and rushes* d. c.)

Bouzin. It's a far far better thing that I do now than I have ever done!

(*The* Police *seize* Bouzin *again and drag him off as the Curtain falls.*)

Everyone. Down to the Station!

CURTAIN

PROPERTY LIST

ACT ONE

Set:

On Stage:
  In dining room—five place servings, five wine glasses, five dinner plates, two decanters of wine, two pieces of French bread.
  On table, with chairs round it D. R.—one copy of the *Figaro.*
  On chest, extreme D. R.—one silver box containing headache powders.
  On top of piano—spare visiting card.
  On table D. S. of sofa—cigar box containing a few cigars, matches in a silver case.

Off Stage Left:
  One large bouquet
  One small bouquet
  One basket of flowers, containing ring in box
  One sheet music manuscript (Bouzin)
  One envelope, two coins (De Chenneviette)
  Two invitation cards (Lucette)

Off Stage Right:
  One hair brush (Bois d'Enghien)

ACT TWO

Set:

On Stage:
  On table D. R.—hair brush, box of pins, push bell (practical)
  In cupboard U. R.—coat hangers
  On table behind screen—bottle of smelling salts, spare ear of corn, handkerchief
  On chaise longue—Fraulein's gloves and bag

Off Stage Left:
  One small bouquet (Bois d'Enghien)

137

One large bouquet of marigolds and ears of corn with pearls round stem (General)

Travelling bag containing Lucette's costume and fan/gun (De Chenneviette)

Salver with visiting cards (Emile)

ACT THREE

SET:

On Stage:

   On armchair D. R.—one pair of shoes, polishing cloth, duster

   On dressing table—brush and comb

   On washstand—soap, flannel, tooth brush and powder

   On hallstand R.—dressing gown, slippers (Lucette's)

   On door L.—practical door bell

Off Stage U. C.:

   One basket of lilies (Flower Boy)

PROPERTY LIST

Personals:

BOIS D'ENGHIEN—Flannel vest (Act Two), Door key (Act Two)

GENERAL—Bracelet in case (Act One), Large gilt visiting card (Act One), Cane (throughout), Invitation card (Act Two)

BOUZIN—Umbrella (throughout), Visiting cards (Act One), Briefcase containing marriage settlement (Act Three), One sheet music manuscript (Act One)

DE FONTANET—Hat, cane, gloves (Act One), One copy *Figaro* (Act One)

LUCETTE—Bag containing gun/fan (Act Three)

DE CHENNEVIETTE—Hat, cane, gloves (Act One), One copy *Figaro* (Act One)

BARONESS—One copy *Figaro* (Act One)

VIVIANNE—Three copies sheet music (Act Three)

FRAULEIN—Gloves and bag (Act Two)

JEAN—Door key (Act Three)

BRIDE and BRIDESMAID—Bouquets (Act Three)

Also By

AUTHOR

title

title

title

SKIN DEEP
Jon Lonoff

Comedy / 2m, 2f / Interior Unit Set

In *Skin Deep,* a large, lovable, lonely-heart, named Maureen Mulligan, gives romance one last shot on a blind-date with sweet awkward Joseph Spinelli; she's learned to pepper her speech with jokes to hide insecurities about her weight and appearance, while he's almost dangerously forthright, saying everything that comes to his mind. They both know they're perfect for each other, and in time they come to admit it.

They were set up on the date by Maureen's sister Sheila and her husband Squire, who are having problems of their own: Sheila undergoes a non-stop series of cosmetic surgeries to hang onto the attractive and much-desired Squire, who may or may not have long ago held designs on Maureen, who introduced him to Sheila. With Maureen particularly vulnerable to both hurting and being hurt, the time is ripe for all these unspoken issues to bubble to the surface.

"Warm-hearted comedy … the laughter was literally show-stopping.
A winning play, with enough good-humored laughs and sentiment to keep you smiling from beginning to end."
- TalkinBroadway.com

"It's a little Paddy Chayefsky, a lot Neil Simon and a quick-witted, intelligent voyage into the not-so-tranquil seas of middle-aged love and dating. The dialogue is crackling and hilarious; the plot simple but well-turned; the characters endearing and quirky; and lurking beneath the merriment is so much heartache that you'll stand up and cheer when the unlikely couple makes it to the inevitable final clinch."
- NYTheatreWorld.Com

WHITE BUFFALO
Don Zolidis

Drama / 3m, 2f (plus chorus)/ Unit Set

Based on actual events, WHITE BUFFALO tells the story of the miracle birth of a white buffalo calf on a small farm in southern Wisconsin. When Carol Gelling discovers that one of the buffalo on her farm is born white in color, she thinks nothing more of it than a curiosity. Soon, however, she learns that this is the ful- fillment of an ancient prophecy believed by the Sioux to bring peace on earth and unity to all mankind. Her little farm is quickly overwhelmed with religious pilgrims, bringing her into contact with a culture and faith that is wholly unfamiliar to her. When a mysterious businessman offers to buy the calf for two million dol- lars, Carol is thrown into doubt about whether to profit from the religious beliefs of others or to keep true to a spirituality she knows nothing about.

COCKEYED
William Missouri Downs

Comedy / 3m, 1f / Unit Set

Phil, an average nice guy, is madly in love with the beautiful Sophia. The only problem is that she's unaware of his existence. He tries to introduce himself but she looks right through him. When Phil discovers Sophia has a glass eye, he thinks that might be the problem, but soon realizes that she really can't see him. Perhaps he is caught in a philosophical hyperspace or dualistic reality or perhaps beautiful women are just unaware of nice guys. Armed only with a B.A. in philosophy, Phil sets out to prove his existence and win Sophia's heart. This fast moving farce is the winner of the HotCity Theatre's GreenHouse New Play Festival. The St. Louis Post-Dispatch called Cockeyed a clever romantic comedy, Talkin' Broadway called it "hilarious," while Playback Magazine said that it was "fresh and invigorating."

Winner!
of the HotCity Theatre GreenHouse New Play Festival

"Rocking with laughter...hilarious...polished and engaging work draws heavily on the age-old conventions of farce: improbable situations, exaggerated characters, amazing coincidences, absurd misunderstandings, people hiding in closets and barely missing each other as they run in and out of doors...full of comic momentum as Cockeyed hurtles toward its conclusion."
- Talkin' Broadway

SAMUELFRENCH.COM